M/V ISLANDER
Resurrection

M/V ISLANDER
Resurrection

a novella

Kevin Parham

PRIA Publishing
P.O. Box 1815 Sagamore Beach,
Massachusetts 02562
www.priapublishing.com

Cover design by Peter O'Connor, *Bespokebookcovers.com*
Edited by Megan Harris and Jared Carew

Back cover image used by permission,
courtesy of Joan Boyken, *mvobsession.com*

Printed in the United States of America
First Printing 2021

Library of Congress Control Number: 2020939203

ISBN: 978-0-9849485-7-4

Publisher's Cataloging-in-Publication Data

Names: Parham, Kevin, author.
Title: MV Islander - Resurrection / Kevin Parham.
Description: Sagamore Beach, MA: Pria Publishing, 2021.
Identifiers: ISBN 978-0-9849485-7-4 (pbk.) |

Subjects: LCSH Adult–Fiction. | Fantasy–Paranormal–Fiction. | Satire–Fiction. | Martha's Vineyard (Mass.)–Fiction. | Massachusetts–Fiction. | Small town & Rural–Fiction. |
United States—20th century–Fiction. | BISAC FICTION / General
Classification: LCC PS3616 .A43125 W47 2021 | DDC 813.6–dc23

This is a work of fiction. Names, characters, businesses, place, and incidents are either the products of the author's imagination or used in a fictitious manner. Any references to historical events or real people are used fictitiously.

Contents

Chapter One

On a mild, sun-splashed morning in June, a frail, elderly woman—hunched over while grabbing hold of a cane for support—walked slowly towards the ticket window at the Commonwealth Ferryboat Company terminal in Woods Hole, Massachusetts.

The clerk at the window, his patience wearing thin, repeatedly tapped a ball-point pen on the countertop as he watched the woman rummage through her pocketbook.

"Can I help you?" he asked.

The woman stepped to the window, and said, in a meek tone, "Yes. I'd like to purchase a ticket to the Vineyard for my car."

"Do you have a reservation?"

"No," she replied.

"I'm sorry, but I can't help you. Today's Friday. There's no standby on Fridays, Saturdays, Sundays, or Mondays during the peak season."

The woman removed her bifocals, brushed her stringy, shoulder-length gray hair from her furrowed face, and said, "There must be something you can do."

"Ma'am, there's nothing I can do," the clerk said.

While attempting to hold back the tears, her eyes welling up and a look of desperation on her face, she turned towards the clerk, and said, in a wavering voice, "But sir, I must get my car to Martha's Vineyard on the next boat. It's my husband. He's in hospice, dying, and I've got to get to him!"

A man who happened to be waiting in line stepped up to the woman, and said, "Excuse me, but I couldn't help overhearing your conversation. I have a reservation booked on the next ferry, and I'm in no hurry to get my car to the island. You can have my reservation."

"Why, thank you, sir. That's very kind of you," she said with a solemn expression.

The ticket clerk snapped to attention, looked at them, and said, "Now wait just a minute. You can't do that, sir. Vehicle reservations *are not transferable*! It's company policy."

"What are you talking about? Where's your sense of decency? Do you not have an iota of compassion for the woman? Her husband's dying, for God's sake," the man said.

The clerk ignored the man's exhortation, waved them aside, and said, in a dismissive tone, "Next! I can help the next person in line."

The man reached for the woman's hand and led her towards the door. He turned, looked at the clerk, and said, "You're a jackass!"

As they walked out of the building, the woman looked at the gentleman, and asked, "What has the Commonwealth Ferryboat Company become? It's nothing like it used to be."

"Indeed," the man concurred.

Three other customers, a woman in her mid-thirties and two older men, while waiting in line for what felt as if it were an eternity, commented on what they had witnessed.

"Can you believe how rude the clerk was to that woman?" the woman asked.

"It's disgusting. If it weren't for the fact that the Commonwealth Ferryboat Company is the only means of getting my truck to and from Martha's Vineyard, I'd choose another boat line in a heartbeat," the first man said.

The second man said, "The problem is that there's no competition to transport vehicles to the Vineyard and Nantucket. The C.F.C. is a monopoly; it's the only game in town. It's been that way since the 1960s."

"Unfortunately, that's correct," the woman replied. "Not to mention the fact that they've got a stranglehold on island commerce."

"Do you think it'll ever change?" the first man asked.

The other two looked at each other, a smirk on their faces, and said, simultaneously, "No way."

"I think you're both right. Not as long as the Massachusetts legislature controls things," the first man conceded.

Chapter Two

When Jacques Windham learned through happenstance that the Commonwealth Ferryboat Company had planned to add a new vessel to its aging fleet to accommodate the anticipated increase in passenger and vehicle traffic, he placed an impromptu telephone call to his old friend and former college classmate, Massachusetts Senate President, William Clay.

"Hello, Bill?" Jacques said.

"Yes?"

"Bill, this is Jacques Windham."

"Jacques Windham? My old college buddy? It's been ages since we've spoken. In fact, the last time I laid eyes on you was over thirty years ago at Harvard's commencement exercises, isn't that right?"

"That would be correct, Bill. I can't believe how quickly time has passed."

"How are you? How's your family?" Bill asked.

"Everyone's fine, thanks. And how are things up there in the northeast?"

"I can't complain. Besides, no one's interested in hearing my woes anyway," Bill joked.

"I understand completely," Jacques said.

Jacques Windham's friendship with William Clay had begun in the 1970s at Harvard University, in Cambridge, Massachusetts. While there, Clay had earned a law degree and pursued a career in Massachusetts politics. Windham, after having earned an MBA, went on to become President and CEO of the Mississippi Dry-Dock Company in Harvey, Louisiana.

"Listen, Bill, I'm calling because I could really use your help with something," Jacques said.

"You need my help, huh? Why, of course, my friend. What can I do for you?" he asked.

"I had heard from a reliable source that the Commonwealth Ferryboat Company plans to go out to bid on the construction of a new vessel. I'm sure it comes as no surprise that my company intends to submit a bid for the contract. As you know, Bill, boat-building is my specialty; that's the business I'm in."

"Yes, I'm aware of that," Bill said.

"Well, seeing that my efforts and generous monetary contribution to your reelection campaign in 2002 was instrumental in helping you win, I was wondering if you'd be so kind as to reciprocate the favor by pulling a few strings, as it were. To be frank with you, Bill, I'm at a point of desperation. It's imperative that the Mississippi Dry-Dock Company wins that ferry contract. We *really* need the business. In fact, the company's survival depends on it. If we can win the contract, we'll be able to stay in business. If not, then it'll be impossible for the company to remain solvent. It's as simple as that," Jacques said.

Bill, while holding the telephone to his ear with his left hand, subconsciously massaged his forehead with the other hand. He thought for a moment, and then said, "Well, Jacques, if I were you, I'd submit a bid as soon as the request for proposals is made public."

"I wholeheartedly agree. But if I were to do that, and, for some reason, happened to lose the bid, I'll have no choice but to file for Chapter 7 bankruptcy. And you know what that'll mean...I'll be forced out of business; all of the company's assets will have to be liquidated. I can't afford to take that chance," Jacques said.

"Jacques, you *do* realize what you're asking me to do is illegal, not to mention the moral and ethical implications I'd have to deal with. Besides it being a violation of the public trust, it also could get us into a boatload of trouble, no pun intended."

Jacques paused, and then said, "I understand. But things are bleak down here in the Bayou. I can barely keep my head above water. Hurricane Katrina wreaked havoc on countless businesses in Louisiana, including mine. Our operation has just about ground to a halt. I'm afraid I have no choice but to call in the favor," Jacques said. "Under normal circumstances, I'd never consider making such a request. But at this point, I have no other choice, Bill. I *really* need that ferry contract. My company will go under if something doesn't come through...and soon!"

Suddenly, an awkward moment of silence had created a void in the conversation. It was deafening.

"Let me see what I can do, Jacques. I'll get back to you in a few days," Bill said.

"Thanks, Bill. I'd really appreciate your help with this."

As soon as Bill lay the telephone down on its cradle, he felt a cold shiver shoot up his spine. On the one hand, he wanted to help his old friend, but there was only so much he could do…legally. And, on the other, he knew he was on the hook after having knowingly accepted illegal cash contributions from Jacques. What's more, he was cognizant of the fact that the money had exceeded the maximum amount allowed for campaign contributions. Overwhelmed by feelings of trepidation, reluctantly, Bill decided to help Jacques. He felt he had no choice. But, at what cost?

Bill was a shrewd politician and knew exactly how to broach a request so as not to appear to cross the line of impropriety. If a request happened to be frowned upon, or rejected, he knew he could always resort to using obscure tidbits of derogatory information to his advantage, information about an individual that would otherwise not be available as a matter of public record.

As senate president, Bill had access to swaths of confidential data about Massachusetts residents that could be used to get what he wanted, even if it meant resorting to coercion as a means to an end.

Next morning, Bill placed a telephone call to Mr. Harold Grandly, Chairman of the Board at the Commonwealth Ferryboat Company.

"Mr. Grandly, I have Massachusetts Senate President William Clay's office on the phone. Shall I transfer the call?" Jane, the secretary, asked.

"Yes, Jane. I'll take it in my office," he said.

Harold hobbled toward his office; his tall, lanky frame mimicked an old, retired basketball player who might have once basked in the glory of NBA stardom. As he walked through the door to his office, his bald head nearly grazed the top of the doorjamb. Once inside, he forcefully closed the door behind him, the hollow sound of the rickety wooden door reverberated throughout the office. Just as Harold sat down at his desk, Jane transferred the call. After the third ring, he picked up the handset.

"Good morning, this is Harold Grandly speaking. How can I help you?" he asked.

"Mr. Grandly, this is Massachusetts Senate President, Bill Clay."

"Hello, Mr. Senate President. It's an honor to speak with you, sir. What can I do for you?"

"Mr. Grandly—"

"Please, senator, call me Harold."

"Very well, then. Harold, I'm calling because I'd like to enlist your help with something that's of great importance to me," he said.

"Why, of course, Mr. Clay. I'd be happy to assist you in any way I can," Harold said.

"Before I begin, I must insist that what we're about to discuss be kept in strict confidence; you are to share this with no one. Do I make myself clear, Harold?"

"Yes, sir, I understand. You have my word."

"Good. Now then, it's my understanding that the Commonwealth Ferryboat Company is about to begin the procurement process to acquire a new vessel to replace the ferry, Islander. Is that true?"

"Yes, that's correct," Harold said.

"Has the C.F.C. Board of Directors formally approved a request for proposals on a contract?"

"Not yet. We'll be discussing that topic at the board meeting next week."

"Perfect timing," the senator said. "Harold, I'd really appreciate it if you would award the contract to the Mississippi Dry-Dock Company in Harvey, Louisiana."

"But senator, the C.F.C. Board of Directors isn't permitted to engage in activities that might place undue influence on the procurement process. Not only would it be highly inappropriate, it's also illegal. I'm sure you're aware of that, sir."

"Yes, I'm well aware of the legalities involved in doing such a thing, Harold. But I also know there are ways to get around obstacles such as this, if you catch my drift."

"I certainly do, senator. But, it's still illegal."

A moment of silence ensued, as if the call had suddenly been disconnected.

Senator Clay said, "Well, Mr. Grandly, if we're going to broach the subject of what's legal and what's not, then I'd go so far as to say that embezzling one-hundred thousand dollars from the C.F.C. coffers and using the money to purchase a new car, home improvements, and family trips to Maui and Europe is also illegal. Wouldn't you agree?"

Harold Grandly was speechless. He was so taken aback by what the senator had said that his body jerked straight up in the chair and stiffened. It was almost as if a steel rod had supplanted the vertebrae in his spine. All he could do was sit there with his mouth gaping open. Clearly disturbed, the telephone almost slipped out of his cold, sweaty hand. Suddenly, a lump formed in his throat; he felt as if he had swallowed a grapefruit, whole. And, as Harold listened to the senate president check-off a laundry-list of nefarious activities that Harold had engaged in over the years, he became anxious and began to perspire. It felt as if a 100-pound barbell was pressing down on his chest, making it almost impossible to breathe.

The senator continued.

"And I won't even discuss how you had bribed a circuit court judge into dismissing three OUI charges against you, or, that you had falsified your federal and state income tax returns for the years 2002, 2003, and 2005."

Realizing the gravity of the situation, Harold began to feel nauseated. He wiped the perspiration from his brow, and then subconsciously whisked the top of his balding head with his fingers, attempting to rearrange the strands of thinning gray hair. And by the time he had had a clear understanding of the consequences of not doing what senator had asked, he could barely utter a response.

Feeling as if he were trapped, and with no way out, Mr. Grandly surmised that he had no choice but to honor the senator's request. The only question was…how? If Harold had refused to comply, then Senator Clay would most likely blow the whistle on him, ensuring that he'd be charged with multiple felonies—something he could ill afford to have to deal with.

Harold had finally composed himself enough to respond. "I'll be happy to do whatever's necessary to accommodate your request, Senator Clay," he said.

"That'll be fine, Harold. I'm glad we were able to come to an understanding. I look forward to speaking with you after the contract is awarded to the Mississippi Dry-Dock Company. Thanks again, and have a wonderful day," the senator said.

Harold's hands began to shake uncontrollably as he hung up the telephone. He stared out his office window and wondered, how *am I going to pull this off without ending up in prison where I'd be digging ditches, collecting trash along a highway, or cracking rocks under the hot summer sun?*

Chapter Three

After the treasurer's report of projected revenues and expenses for the next three years had been presented at the quarterly C.F.C. board meeting, a somber silence permeated the conference room. John de Souza, a short and stocky fair-skinned man with a dark-brown crew-cut and bushy mustache, wearing khaki slacks, a white-collared shirt, and oxblood loafers, sat stoic in his chair as he waited to hear the inevitable. Much to his dismay, the financial report was worse than he had anticipated. And, as general manager at the Commonwealth Ferryboat Company, the news hit him like a ton of bricks. In fact, his face had turned an ashy gray, as if all the blood had been drained from his head.

"Mr. de Souza, after having heard the treasurer's report, I'm sure you can see the need to increase operating revenues. Though the C.F.C.'s profit margins have increased by three percent annually, costs have skyrocketed by more than ten percent. At that rate, the C.F.C. will soon be at risk of insolvency, and you know what that'll mean. We'll have no choice but to cut operating expenses, and that will most certainly include layoffs," said Harold Grandly, Chairman of the Commonwealth Ferryboat Company Board of Directors.

Suddenly, John raised his eyebrows and winced, almost as if he'd been poked by a Taser.

An expression of dismay on his face, he said, "Yes, I understand, Mr. Grandly. But I can assure you that the management team is doing everything possible to reduce costs. In fact, I'll have several recommendations to present to the board next week," John said.

"Perhaps we could hire a consulting firm and roll out a new advertising campaign that will bolster ridership," another board member suggested.

"Ridership isn't the problem," Mr. Grandly said. "Most of the spaces on the ferries have already been booked for the entire season, including the holiday weekends of Memorial Day, the Fourth of July, and Labor Day. The real culprit is the cost of maintenance; it's through the roof. Our entire fleet is aging, the motor vessel Islander, in particular. She's on her third set of engines, and we're being nickel and dimed each time she's taken out of service for maintenance. That ferry is like a big hole in the ocean that we keep tossing money into."

"True. But she's the most reliable vessel in the fleet, and need I say, the most beloved," John said.

"Perhaps you're right, John. But, throwing away money just to keep her running for a few more years isn't cost effective. In fact, it's just plain stupid."

Mr. Grandly looks at the board members seated around the conference table, and says, "Do any of you have a suggestion as to what we should do about this dilemma?"

A board member chimes in. "As much as we admire the Islander, I think it's time we consider replacing her with a new vessel. What's more, if we want to attract more business and increase revenues, we'll need a bigger boat."

"And, in order to cut costs, we're going to have to stop bleeding red ink. The only logical solution is to move ahead with a plan to acquire a new ferry," a second board member said.

When the suggestion to purchase a new ferry was proffered, John felt as if he had been kicked in the stomach. Somehow, the Islander's deterioration and exorbitant maintenance costs were immaterial to him. Though his *real* reason for wanting to keep the old vessel in the C.F.C. fleet was personal, his attempt to justify it had fallen on deaf ears; the board of directors would hear none of it.

John had always had a special admiration for the Islander. Having grown up on Martha's Vineyard, the ferry had been an integral part of his childhood. He felt fortunate to have been aboard her countless times over the course of five decades. To him, the Islander wasn't just a floating hunk of steel, glass, and diesel fuel. Rather, she was almost like a member of the family, or, a protective guardian you could always rely on to get you safely across Vineyard Sound in all types of weather.

Throughout the years, John couldn't help but feel enamored by the Islander. As a young boy, he used to ride his bicycle to the wharf in Vineyard Haven almost every day during summers to watch the ferry arrive and unload passengers and vehicles, only to load up again and depart thirty minutes later. He'd even hang around the wharf for hours and watch the C.F.C. employees perform their tasks.

And during the school year, while day-dreaming as he sat at his desk in class at Martha's Vineyard Regional High School, John would subconsciously doodle and draw sketches of the Islander on pads of notepaper or book covers made from brown paper bags. He even built a miniature replica of the ferry out of wood, cardboard, wire mesh, and nails and painted it white. Finally, he completed the model with the signature black stripe that spanned the length of the ferry where the windows were positioned on each side. John used to dream about one day working for the Commonwealth Ferryboat Company. That way, he'd never be far from his beloved Islander. His obsession with the ferry and ultimate career path were a self-fulfilling prophecy.

John raised his hand and requested permission to address the board of directors. Having been recognized by the chairman, John stood up, and said, "Before taking a final vote on this proposal, I'd respectfully ask you to consider upgrading the Islander instead of replacing her. After all, she's paid for. And what would it cost to build a new vessel?" John asked.

"It'll cost approximately thirty-two million dollars, Mr. de Souza. That's what we've been quoted for a vessel that'll meet our needs," Mr. Grandly said.

"With all due respect, Mr. Grandly, how could you possibly know the cost of a new vessel before you've received bids from prospective shipbuilders? Has the C.F.C. submitted a request for proposals?"

Based on body language, several board members appeared to have been taken aback by John's pointed questions. They glanced at one another and waited for Mr. Grandly to respond.

"John, we've mulled over this issue for quite some time, close to a year, in fact. And, in the process, we've conducted an exhaustive amount of research with the understanding that the Islander would eventually have to be replaced," Mr. Grandly said.

"But..."

"I'd like to make a motion to solicit bids on a new ferry," Mr. Grandly proposed. All in favor—say aye."

"Aye," said four members of the board.

"Second?"

"Second!" another board member said.

"All opposed?"

There was no response.

"The 'ayes' have it; the motion is carried. Mr. de Souza, please be advised that the C.F.C. Board will convene a public hearing in two weeks to announce our intention to replace the Islander with a new ferry. And please let your management team know of this decision immediately," Mr. Grandly said. "Also, we'll need to issue a public notice announcing the day and time of the hearing. Jane, please see that it's published in the local newspapers, including *The Martha's Vineyard Times*, *Vineyard Gazette*, and The *Cape Cod Times*. Also, please ensure that the notice is posted at all town halls, libraries, and public buildings on the Vineyard and Nantucket."

The board's secretary, Jane, said, "Yes, sir," as she continued to take copious notes of the meeting.

In the ten years that John had been a general manager at the Commonwealth Ferryboat Company, he had never felt so discouraged. In his heart, he knew that the C.F.C. Board's action would not sit well with many island residents. But, fiscally, it made sense; for, attempting to maintain a vessel that's over fifty years old is a fool's proposition.

John arrived at home just after 6:00 p.m. Feeling disconsolate and emotionally drained, he slowly trudged up the cobblestone sidewalk, a pensive look on his face, opened a rickety wooden gate, and walked along a path that led to the front door.

He hardly noticed the chill in the air as he approached. It was only after he'd seen the condensation from his hot breath slowly float upwards that he'd become cognizant of how cold it was outside.

The house where John and his wife, Elisa, resided—an old, wooden saltbox surrounded by a white, paint-chipped picket fence and covered by weathered cedar shingles—was in serious disrepair. Despite this, John and Elisa were proud of their home. The house—once owned by a whaling captain in the 1800s—was listed in the historical register as one of the stops along the Underground Railroad. At one time, it served as a temporary refuge for African Americans who had escaped slavery in the south.

John and Elisa, having been married for twenty-two years, were without children and lived an imperturbable life. They had known each other since grade school, and, consequently, had become childhood sweethearts. While in high school, John and Elisa were inseparable. They had attended the junior and senior proms together and it had gotten to a point where you never saw one without the other.

While growing up, Elisa lived a bucolic existence. She was raised on an up-island farm, one of eight siblings, and was somewhat of a homebody—shy, with a small circle of friends and limited social engagement. After she had graduated from high school, she obtained a job as a cashier at a grocery store in West Tisbury. A few years afterwards, she was offered the position of store manager, a job she continued to hold.

John, on the other hand, was an only child. Because of that, he felt the need to look outside his family for social interaction. His outgoing personality made it easy for him to make friends. When presented with an opportunity to work as a general manager at the Commonwealth Ferryboat Company, he eagerly accepted the position.

When John walked into the house, almost immediately he knew what Elisa had prepared for dinner. The hearty aroma of a pot roast and the sweet scent of fresh vegetables—lightly seasoned with basil, rosemary, and thyme—wafted through the air and tantalized John's olfactory nerves. There was no mistaking the familiar smell of succulent ingredients simmering in a cast-iron pot in the oven.

Before John got to the kitchen, he stopped in the hallway. While there, he inhaled the rich fragrances that made his mouth water as he anticipated the wonderful meal in which he would soon partake.

Elisa was a petite woman, about five-foot-three inches tall. Her curly, light-brown hair resembled a combination of a bouffant and a beehive. She stood at the counter and fumbled with a potato ricer that she was attempting to use to make garlic mashed potatoes.

"Hello, dear; it's sure good to be home," John said as he gave his wife an affectionate peck on the cheek.

Elisa stopped, placed the potato ricer down on the counter, and said with a smile, "Hi, John. How was your day?"

John looks at her with a solemn expression, and says, "All I can say is that I've had better days."

"Why? What happened?" she asked.

Before answering, John walked over to the stove, opened the oven door, and peered inside. He then bent down to smell the wonderful aroma wafting from the roast as it slowly cooked in a thick, bubbling brown gravy.

"Well, for starters, the C.F.C. board meeting was quite contentious," he said.

"Really? Why?"

"The board of directors came down hard on the management team. They want us to cut operating costs. Again. Heck, we've already trimmed the excess fat down to the bone. It's becoming untenable. All they seem to care about is the bottom line. Revenue, revenue, revenue. That's all I ever hear. They obviously don't give a damn about customer service. The term 'customer satisfaction' doesn't seem to be part of their vernacular anymore. The Commonwealth Ferryboat Company is supposed to be a not-for-profit entity, but you'd never know it by the way they're managing things," John said.

"What's so unusual about that? Isn't that the way it's always been?"

"I suppose so. But for some reason, the tone of the meeting seemed different. It was almost as if the board felt a collective sense of urgency. And, to top it off, they're going to hold a public hearing in two weeks," he said.

"A public hearing? What in God's name for?"

"It seems that they're hell-bent on replacing the Islander."

"Seriously?"

"Yes," he said.

Elisa paused, and then began to set the table for dinner. As John gazed out the kitchen window, he seemed lost in thought, almost as if he were in a trance. He looks down at the table and notices three place settings, instead of the usual two.

"What's with the three plate settings? Are we having company for dinner?" John asked.

"Oh, I meant to tell you. My brother, Ralph, arrived unexpectedly on the island today and I invited him to dinner."

"Ralph? Ralph's here on the island? But it's January; He *never* comes to the Vineyard in winter. What's he doing here now?"

"Says he's here on business, something about negotiating a contract," she said.

"Contract? What contract? And why on earth would he come to Martha's Vineyard to negotiate a contract in the dead of winter?"

"I don't know. But I'm sure we'll find out when he gets here," she said.

At 7:00 p.m., Elisa's brother arrived at the house and knocked lightly on the front door. John opened the door and Ralph walked inside, sporting a wide smile and an outstretched hand. John grabbed hold of Ralph's hand, gave him a firm handshake and embraced him.

"Hello there, Ralph. What a surprise it is to see you," John said, a curious expression on his face.

"Greetings, John! Hi, Sis! How in the heck are you two doin'? I can't tell you how happy I am to see y'all," Ralph said, with a slight southern drawl as he took off his grey three-quarter length wool coat, painter's cap, and matching leather gloves and hung them on a coat tree by the door. Short stature was an attribute in Elisa's family; Ralph wasn't much taller than his sister. His narrow facial features and hook nose appeared more pronounced under the opaque light in the hallway.

"Come, Ralph," Elisa said as she grabbed his hand and led him to the kitchen. "John almost didn't believe me when I told him you were on the island."

"That's correct. I didn't. You've never come to the Vineyard in the wintertime," John said.

"True. I didn't plan to come. But my boss insisted that I accompany him on this trip. You see, we're here to meet with a client about building a new vessel," Ralph said.

"Who's the client?" John asked.

"I don't know; it all happened so fast. What I do know is that the company is on Cape Cod. However, it's my understanding that the person we're meeting lives on the Vineyard. It's an exploratory meeting; nothing's been finalized yet. We're only here to negotiate, that's all."

Suddenly, the wheels in John's head began to spin. He couldn't help but think there might be a connection between the C.F.C. Board's plan to acquire a new ferry and Ralph's employer, the Mississippi Dry-Dock Company. Surely, if Ralph had known that his company was negotiating a contract with the Commonwealth Ferryboat Company, surely, he'd tell John. Or, would he? Just as John's suspicions were about to go into overdrive, Elisa said, "Dinner's ready, let's eat!"

They sat down at a white, rectangular Formica table. Based on the number of nicks, gashes, and scratches it contained, it was easy to tell that the table had seen many years of use. Elisa served the food, and the three of them indulged in a delectable meal. After they had finished the main course, Ralph said, "I'll tell you something, Sis. I know of *no one* who can cook a sumptuous meal like you can."

"Why, thank you, Ralph—you're much too kind," she said, blushing slightly.

"So, Ralph, when and where is your meeting?" John asked.

"Tomorrow morning, at the Harbor View Hotel in Edgartown," he said.

"Are you staying at the hotel tonight?" Elisa asked.

"Yes."

"How long will you be on the island?" John asked.

"My boss and I have to leave tomorrow morning, right after the meeting. Because of business demands, we've got to get back to Louisiana as soon as possible," he said.

"I'm sorry you have to leave the island so soon," Elisa said.

"So am I. But a man's gotta earn a living!" he replied, with a wide grin that displayed his front buck teeth, pearly-white, with a slight overbite.

"I hope you gentlemen haven't eaten so much that you don't have room for dessert."

"Dessert? What is it?" Ralph asked.

"Devil's food cake with chocolate fudge frosting and French vanilla ice cream," she said.

"Now, how could we say no to that?" John said.

"Mmm...that sounds good. Bring it on, Sis!" Ralph said, as he licked his lips.

Dinner ended just after 9:00 p.m. Shortly thereafter, John and Ralph retired to the comfort of the living room where two oversized, green easy chairs—padded with fluffy, beige cushions—seemed to invite them to come over and sit down. While there, they smoked cigars and sipped Brandy as the song; T*ake the A-Train* by Duke Ellington, played softly in the background. About an hour later, Ralph stood, and said, "Well, I'd best be going, John. I can't thank you and Elisa enough for your hospitality. Dinner was delicious, and the company delightful, as always!"

"You are more than welcome, Ralph," John said. "And good luck tomorrow."

"Thanks, John."

Elisa walked into the living room just as Ralph and John were heading towards the front door.

"Goodbye, Sis…I'll call you next Sunday," Ralph said as he grabbed his coat, hat, and gloves from the coat tree.

"Okay, Ralph. Goodbye…I love you," said Elisa.

"Thanks, Sis. And I love you, too," he said as he gave her a warm embrace.

Ralph gave John a firm handshake. He then slipped on his coat, hat, and gloves, and then walked out the door and made his way to a rented silver-gray Honda FIT.

After Ralph had driven away, John thought about the impromptu visit and how unusual it was. In fact, it weighed heavily on his mind; so much so, it had gotten to a point where he could no longer keep his thoughts to himself. And as he and Elisa were getting ready for bed, he said, "I suspect Ralph's meeting tomorrow has something to do with the new ferry the C.F.C. plans to purchase."

"What makes you think that?" she asked.

"I don't know. It's just a hunch."

"Why didn't you ask Ralph about it when he was here?"

"Two reasons: first, I didn't want it to seem like I was prying into his business. And second, I'd feel embarrassed if it turns out to be true and I knew nothing about it. He'd think I was an incompetent fool," John said.

"Isn't the C.F.C. required by law to solicit bids for a project of that size?" Elisa asked.

"They are. But I wouldn't be surprised if they're somehow involved in shenanigans to circumvent the bidding process," he said.

He reached for the lamp on the nightstand and turned off the light.

“But wouldn’t that be illegal?” Elisa asked.

“Yes, it would. But you’d be appalled by what goes on at the C.F.C., particularly when it involves politics.”

After lying awake in bed for almost an hour, John rolled over and finally drifted off to sleep.

Chapter Four

The following morning, John decided to act on a hunch. He hopped out of bed, took a shower, got dressed, and then drove to the Harbor View Hotel in Edgartown. When he arrived, he parked alongside the curb about one hundred and fifty feet from the front entrance. Wanting to remain inconspicuous, he sat slouched down in the driver's seat and watched people go in and come out of the hotel. At approximately 10:15 a.m., his brother-in-law, Ralph, Mr. Grandly, and another gentleman, most likely Ralph's boss, walked out of the hotel and shook hands on the sidewalk before going their separate ways. John's suspicions, having now been confirmed, made him feel sick to his stomach.

John sat in his car and attempted to rationalize the incredulousness of what he had just witnessed. Moments later, he drove away from the hotel and headed to his office in Vineyard Haven, eight miles away.

After having navigated his car into a small parking lot next to the wharf, John got out and walked towards the ticket office. The pungent odor of marine diesel oil lingered in the air, and the rumbling sound from engines on a departing freight barge had temporarily distracted John from what had been weighing heavily on his mind.

"Mornin', Mr. de Souza," said Shirley Dupree, a C.F.C. employee who worked as a custodian at the ticket office. Shirley, a short and burley, olive-skinned woman with flaming red, shoulder-length hair and with barely a tenth-grade education, had acquired her job through a friend of her cousin, who also happened to work for the C.F.C. What was notable about Shirley was that she hadn't missed a day of work in over seven years.

"Good morning, Shirley. How's the family?" John asked.

"Everyone's doin' fine," she said. "Looks like it's fixin' to be another hectic day, you reckon?"

"Yes, yes, I agree," John said as he began to climb the stairs to his office on the second floor.

While sitting at his desk, John wondered whether he should ask Mr. Grandly about what he had witnessed at the Harbor View Hotel earlier that morning. He believed that the bidding process had been compromised but was at a loss as to how it could have happened without his knowledge. After mulling it over, he thought it best to remain mum for fear of receiving a stern rebuke from Mr. Grandly, or worse, being fired from his job. To get the issue off his mind, he grabbed the C.F.C. financial report from his desk and began to read it.

After carefully reviewing the maintenance logs for the past twelve months, John could hardly believe his eyes. The exorbitant cost of repairs to the vessels was shocking; so much so, it made him toss the report to the floor. And for the next eight hours, he hunkered down at the office and dealt with a myriad of issues at the Vineyard Haven ferry terminal.

At the end of what was an extraordinarily long and unproductive day, John walked out of the office, hopped into his car, and headed for home. Even while in the comfort of familiar surroundings, still, he couldn't seem to shake off his solemn mood.

John sat down at the kitchen table and was unusually quiet. Elisa looked at him, and said, "Don't tell me you're still brooding over the C.F.C.'s decision to replace the Islander."

"And what if I am?" he asked in a disgruntled tone.

"Well, if you are, then I'd suggest you get over it. Besides, I thought you had agreed with the decision."

"I *did* agree. But it's not so much the decision that bothers me; it's the manner in which the board members had come to it. I still think that they engaged in underhanded tactics to circumvent the bidding process."

"How do you know that to be true?"

"I don't know for sure; it's just a feeling I have."

"Do you plan to attend the hearing?" She asked.

"You couldn't keep me away even if you hog-tie and chain me to the dock. You can bet I'll be there. Would you care to join me?" he asked.

"Of course, I'll join you," she said.

During the time leading up to the hearing, John didn't mention to anyone—including his wife—about his sneaking suspicion that a contract had been signed by the Commonwealth Ferryboat Company and the Mississippi Dry-Dock Company. In fact, he avoided telling Elisa out of concern for the discord it might cause. At times, John felt as if he were about to explode from anger, but he didn't utter a word.

Two weeks later, on a blustery February evening, a public hearing was held at the C.F.C. administration offices in Woods Hole. The meeting room was packed with more than one hundred people. Every seat was occupied. As a result, John and Elisa had to stand at the back of the room. More than likely, this would be the only opportunity for concerned citizens to voice their opinion for or against the proposed plan to retire the Islander and replace her with a new ferry.

The C.F.C. Board of Directors sat around a polished mahogany table and watched several attendees jockey for a limited number of folding metal chairs that had been brought in and haphazardly placed at the back of the room.

Mr. Grandly gaveled the meeting to order.

"Good evening everyone. On behalf of the C.F.C. Board of Directors, I'd like to thank you for taking time to be here tonight. The purpose of this meeting is to gather commentary about a proposal to upgrade the C.F.C.'s fleet. As you know by now, we plan to replace the motor vessel Islander with a new, more efficient ferry. In that regard, we invite you to share your opinions about the board's proposed plan. For those who would like to make a comment, you'll have up to three minutes to do so," Mr. Grandly said.

A wave of people rushed to the front of the room and stood in a long line that extended out the rear door. Tensions were high; you could almost feel the apprehension in the room. The first person to speak, a meek-looking middle-age, muscular white man with a balding head, wearing farmer jeans, a red and blue lumberjack shirt, and dingy, mud-laced work boots, stepped up to the microphone.

"My name's Vincent Franklin, a life-long resident of Tisbury. And as you can see, I'm a farmer; third generation, in fact. I've been so ever since I was old enough to hold a rake. Now what y'all are proposin' to do here is just plain stupid. It's a waste of money. I don't want to have to pay higher prices to get my produce to market just because you want to get rid of the Islander and replace her with somethin' that'll bankrupt us all. The Islander suits me just fine—you should find a way to keep her. I think y'all should reconsider y'all's decision."

"Thank you for sharing your thoughts with us, Mr. Franklin," Mr. Grandly said.

A petit, African American woman with a cocoa-brown complexion and shoulder-length dark brown hair, smartly dressed in a navy-blue pants-suit, light green blouse and matching blue high heeled shoes, approached the microphone. Her jade-colored eyes focused on the board members like a laser, prompting several of them to avoid eye contact by looking down at the table, or up towards the ceiling.

"Good evening. My name is Rebecca Cartwright, Oak Bluffs Town Administrator. As someone who's intimately connected not only to the residents of Oak Bluffs, but also to the five other towns on Martha's Vineyard, I can assure you that the path you're embarking on does not sit well with a large swath of your constituency. I know this to be true; I hear about it almost every day," she said.

"That's all well and good, Ms. Cartwright—"

"Mrs. Cartwright," she said, interrupting the board chairman.

"I apologize, Mrs. Cartwright. As I was about to say, the board had decided that, based on an in-depth, independent study, the best course of action to take would be to purchase a new vessel," Mr. Grandly said.

"Regardless of what you claim to be true, Mr. Chairman, the numbers simply don't add up," she retorted.

Suddenly, a man sitting down at the back of the room, stood up from his chair, and yelled out, "Who do you clowns think you're foolin'? Everyone here knows this is nothin' but a sham! If you think you can railroad, hoodwink, or bamboozle us into believing this crock o' shit you're dishing out, then you've got another think comin'," he said.

A board member perked up and said, "Excuse me, sir, but we didn't catch your name."

"Hennessy. The name's Jack Hennessy, spelled the same as the cognac. And I'm 100-proof pissed-off at you jokers."

"The board can appreciate your passion regarding this issue, Mr. Hennessey," Mr. Grandly said.

"Yeah, whatever," Mr. Hennessey said.

An elderly man, a WWII Veteran, sporting a well-preserved Army uniform, decorated with several metals of honor, walked slowly up to the microphone. He looked around the room, and then at the board members, and said, "I was born on the Martha's Vineyard. I proudly served my country during the war. Throughout my entire life, I traveled on the Islander. I love the old ferry; she's like a member of my family, and I implore you not to scrap her."

"What is your name, sir?"

"Lieutenant Raymond Smith."

"We thank you for your service, Lieutenant Smith. You are an American hero," Mr. Grandly said.

For two and a half hours, people stepped up to the microphone and elucidated as to why they did, or did not, support the C.F.C. plan. After the last person had spoken, the consensus was crystal clear. Mr. Grandly did all he could to maintain his game-face, but, whether he realized it or not, his discontent had shown through like an open book, or a laser beam through clear glass.

"On behalf of the C.F.C Board of Director's, I'd like to thank all of you for sharing your thoughts with us about our proposal. You can rest assured that your comments will be taken under advisement as we consider our final decision about the fate of the Islander. I hereby declare this meeting adjourned," Mr. Grandly said with a strike of a gavel.

Chapter Five

At 8:44 p.m., John and Elisa boarded the Islander for what was expected to be a slow, solemn trip back to the Vineyard. And as they sailed across Vineyard Sound, John couldn't help but recount the many years of fond memories riding aboard the old ferry, only to be reminded that the stalwart vessel's days were numbered. He feared it wouldn't be long before the Islander ended up in some distant ship-graveyard.

When they arrived home, they went to the living room and sat down. John clasped his hands and briskly rubbed them together in an attempt to ward off the evening chill. As they sat there, Elisa noticed the message light blinking on the telephone answering machine. She pressed the 'play' button and put it on loudspeaker.

Hello, John, this is Sinclair. I've just received word that the C.F.C. Board took a vote after the hearing tonight and decided to move forward with the purchase of a new ferry. The vote was unanimous, 5 to 0. I'm sorry to have to break the news to you. As you can imagine, the entire crew of the Islander is very disappointed. There's also talk of putting the vessel up for sale. However, if there are no takers, then, most likely, she'll be scrapped. I know this isn't what you wanted to hear; none of us did. But I thought you'd want to know as soon as possible. Let's discuss it in the morning. Thanks.

"Who's Sinclair?" Elisa asked.

"He's the captain of the Islander. I can only imagine how hard this must have hit him."

Elisa grabbed hold of her husband's hand, and said, "Try not to let this upset you, John. I know what the Islander has meant to you; it's always been a part of your life. But things change, and I guess we have to accept the fact that this is one of those times."

"I suppose you're right, Elisa. But still, it's a hard pill to swallow."

Elisa watched her husband as he stared out the living room window. Unsure of what else to say, she got up from the sofa, stretched her arms upward, yawned, and then headed toward the hallway.

"I have to leave for work early tomorrow morning. We're conducting an audit of the inventory at the store. So, I think I'll call it a night. Are you coming to bed, John?" She asked as she made her way to the stairs.

"No, Elisa. You go ahead. I'm going to stay downstairs for a while longer. I'll be up in a few."

John felt himself sinking to the depths of despair. He plopped himself down in the easy chair and, mumbling softly to himself, said, "I could use a drink." He got up, walked over to the cabinet and grabbed hold of a bottle of Jack Daniel's whiskey and a Brandy snifter. He made his way to the kitchen, bottle and snifter in hand, plucked three ice cubes from the freezer and tossed them into the snifter. He poured the whiskey and watched a thin stream of the gold-colored liquid slowly flow into the snifter. Being careful not to spill his libation, John held the snifter as steady as he could as he crept back to the living room. He then dimmed the lights and sat down. Within minutes, he had gulped the whiskey as if it were a glass of water. Shortly thereafter, he refilled the snifter—several times. And for two hours, John sat there and wallowed in self-pity. Eventually, he had drunk himself into a stupor.

The next morning, John arrived to work early. And, despite his having a pounding headache, he prepared for the weekly meeting with his management team. Agenda items included the C.F.C.'s plan to retire the Islander and the acquisition of the new ferry.

While John sat at his desk, the telephone rang. He glanced at a clock on the wall that resembled a ship's porthole and took note of the time: 6:15 a.m. *Now who could be calling at this hour of the morning?* he wondered. At first, he thought it was Elisa, but then realized she would have called his cell phone.

"Hello, John de Souza speaking. How can I help you?"

"John? It's Ralph."

"Ralph? What's going on? Is everything all right?"

After a brief pause, Ralph said, "John, I've got to share something that's been gnawing at me ever since I left the Vineyard two weeks ago."

"What is it, Ralph?"

Ralph pauses again.

He then let out a short, breathy sigh. "John, when my boss, Mr. Lugar, and I traveled to the Vineyard to discuss a potential contract with a new client, I had no idea who the client was. I had told you that the night before the meeting. Do you remember?"

"Yes, I remember," John said.

"Well, the following morning, at the Harbor View Hotel, my boss and I met with Mr. Grandly. And when I learned that he was chairman of the board at the Commonwealth Ferryboat Company and was there to execute a contract for our services, I was taken aback. In fact, the contract was signed by Mr. Grandly and Mr. Lugar that morning. At the time, I was sworn to secrecy. But for the past two weeks, guilt has been tormenting me like you couldn't imagine. John, this is why I'm calling you this morning. You're my sister's husband and my brother-in-law. I simply couldn't betray your trust any longer. The bottom line is that the C.F.C. awarded the construction contract for the new ferry to the Mississippi Dry-Dock Company."

"How is that possible? The C.F.C. hadn't solicited a request for proposals on a contract," John said.

"I don't know," Ralph said, in a muted tone.

"Sounds to me like there's some fishy, back-room dealing going on at the C.F.C.," John said.

"I suspect that the CEO of my company, Jacques Windham, has a connection with someone who's very powerful in Massachusetts government. He must. Because I can't think of any other way that this could have happened," Ralph said.

"Those dirty bastards! I'd bet Mr. Grandly has his hands in the mix," John said.

"Listen, John. You've got to promise not to pursue this matter. Don't say anything to anyone. And *please* don't give Mr. Grandly a reason to think that I had mentioned any of this to you. I could lose my job if whoever's behind this malfeasance discovers that I had tipped you off about it."

"I won't say anything, Ralph. You have my word."

"Thanks, John. I'm really sorry that this happened," Ralph said.

"Not to worry, Ralph," John replied. "It's not your fault. Take care of yourself and thanks for the call."

John stared blankly at the wall, and then placed the telephone on the receiver. He was livid. He could feel his blood pressure rise with each beat of his heart. It had gotten to a point where the repetitive pounding in his head felt like a jackhammer cutting through black asphalt, about to explode.

Prior to going to the conference room, John tossed a couple of aspirin in his mouth and washed them down with water. He wondered whether what felt like a migraine headache was the result of overindulgence the night before, or, a reaction to Ralph's revelation. When he walked into the conference room, it was as if he had entered a wake at a funeral home. Everyone in the room appeared to be in a somber mood.

"Good morning," he said, as he sat down at the head of the table.

"What's so damn good about it?" one of the managers responded, causing others to chuckle.

"It's good to hear some levity, given the circumstances," John said.

"I can't understand why everyone's so glum. It's just a friggin' boat, for God's sake!" the dock manager, Mike Malloy, said.

"Right, Mike. To you, the Islander might be just a hunk of WWII surplus steel, but, to some of us, she's much more than that," John countered.

"I'd suggest we accept the fact that a change is coming. *That* much we can be sure of," Mike said.

"Okay, so what's the plan, John?" asked Mary Worthier, the office supervisor.

John glanced at some notes he had scribbled on a yellow legal pad, and said, "Here's what's going to happen: Last night, the board of directors voted to put the Islander up for sale. And, from what I understand, the New York Port Authority has expressed an interest in purchasing her."

"So soon? That was quite expedient," said Ronald Coombs, the freight manager.

"When can we expect to take delivery of the new ferry?"

"The vessel is due to arrive at the end of the year, around December 31st," John said.

"New Year's Eve?"

"Yes," John said.

"What's the name of the shipbuilder that won the contract?"

"I hope to find out by the end of the day," John replied, even though he already knew.

"Have they decided on a name for the new ferry?" Mary asked.

"The Board is going to solicit the public for suggestions on a name. They think that by getting outside input, perhaps those who are opposed to the idea of replacing the Islander might find it more acceptable," John said.

"I doubt it'll make a difference, despite the overwhelming rejection of the idea that we had witnessed at the hearing. I find it odd that the Board of Directors would be so insolent as to dismiss the will of the people and move ahead with the project anyway," Richard said.

"I agree," Mike said.

"May I continue?" John asked as he impatiently looked

around the room. "When the new vessel arrives, she'll undergo a three-week trial run. Then, after the Coast Guard completes its inspection, the Islander will be decommissioned and transferred to a shipyard in Groton, Connecticut. From there—provided the sale to the New York Port Authority goes through—she'll be brought to New York," John explained.

"Should be interesting," another manager said.

"Okay, folks, that'll be all for now," John said. "Have a great day, and I'll see you out there on the front lines."

The management team filed out of the conference room, and John went back to his office. While there, he again mulled over whether to confront Mr. Grandly about what he knew, even though he had given his word to Ralph that he wouldn't broach the subject. After having considered it further, John thought it best not to show his hand at this time for the sake of his job, and for Ralph's.

Chapter Six

Memorial Day weekend marks the beginning of the summer season at the Commonwealth Ferryboat Company. And with thousands of passengers traveling to and from Martha's Vineyard and Nantucket, a plethora of issues must be dealt with each day, not least of which includes high expectations and the occasional discord that might occur between customers and C.F.C. employees.

The planet Mercury happened to be in retrograde on the Friday before the holiday weekend, and it seemed to have affected the temperament of those who might have been teetering on the cusp of psychosis. As a result, any altercations between customers and C.F.C. employees had the potential to become contentious.

The ticket office in Woods Hole was crowded almost from the time it opened at 5:30 a.m. And it just so happened that three tour buses had simultaneously arrived from Boston, New York City, and Philadelphia. Four C.F.C. shuttle buses—packed with passengers who had parked their cars at several offsite lots—sped down a hill that led to the ferry dock before coming to an abrupt stop behind the tour buses at the terminal. It seemed as if all at once, scores of passengers stepped off the buses and converged upon the ticket office while cars and trucks quickly filled the staging area—each vying to be at the head of the line to board the first ferry to the Vineyard.

A driver on one of the shuttle buses, a young man about twenty-four years old, and two passengers—one male and one female—were embroiled in a heated verbal exchange as they stepped off the C.F.C. shuttle bus.

The male passenger, a rotund, older gentleman, gray-haired, wearing blue jeans, a red lumberjack shirt, cowboy boots and matching hat, said to the driver, "I'll see to it that your driver's license is revoked."

"Oh, yeah? Go ahead and try it—I dare ya. Drivin' this damn bus ain't nothin' but a summer job to me. So, go right ahead and be my guest," the driver snipped.

A Massachusetts State Police Officer on duty at the dock happened to notice the confrontation and approached the three people.

"What's going on here?" the officer asked.

A short, petit woman with shoulder-length dusty-brown hair, green eyes, and a narrow face that possessed a striking resemblance to a hawk, stepped forward and answered, "Officer, first of all, the bus was overcrowded. It felt as if we were livestock being taken to a slaughterhouse. And second, this man is a reckless driver. He shouldn't be allowed to operate motor vehicles, particularly one that transports passengers. Not only did he ignore the speed limit, his wonton disregard for safety had almost caused us bodily harm. In addition to being crammed into the bus like sardines, we had to stand for the entire trip and hold on for dear life while we were tossed around inside the bus. This maniac drove so fast, it felt as if the bus rounded corners on two wheels!"

"She's right," another passenger said. "What's more, this little whippersnapper is a disrespectful son-of-a-bitch."

"All right, everyone. Let's calm down," the officer said.

At that point, the other passengers had already stepped off the bus, grabbed their luggage from the storage compartment below, and made their way to the ticket office. The bus driver wrenched his face, turned and climbed back on to the bus. He plopped himself down in the driver's seat and quickly closed the doors in an attempt to put the confrontation he had had with the two passengers behind him.

Although three ticket windows in the ferry terminal were open for business, they couldn't handle the onslaught of customers standing in long lines, waiting to purchase tickets. Within minutes, the lines had grown to where they stretched out the back door.

Later that morning, a middle-age woman, about five-foot-five, with long, curly, salt and pepper hair and olive-colored skin, stood at one of the ticket windows. She seemed disgruntled about not being able to make a reservation for her car.

"How can you sit there and tell me that I can't get my car to the Vineyard today? Not five minutes ago, I was on the telephone with the reservation office in Mashpee, and, they said I could book a reservation on the nine, eleven, or twelve noon ferry," she said to a middle-aged, portly gentleman sitting behind the counter. He appeared sleepy-eyed and disheveled, as if he'd just crawled out of bed.

"Well, that was five minutes ago, and 'round here, that's an eternity," the clerk said as he rudely yawned in the woman's face and stretched both arms up toward the ceiling. "Things change really fast 'round here."

"Are you trying to tell me that all of the spaces on three ferries have been booked? In five minutes?"

"Let me check again," the clerk said, in a condescending tone. The scowl on his face expressed his discontent. He had made it known to everyone within earshot that the woman had interrupted his breakfast. Before the clerk had so much as lifted a finger, he grabbed hold of a Styrofoam coffee cup and took a sip. He then placed the cup down on the counter, and while holding a blueberry muffin with both hands—similar to a squirrel grasping its food—he quickly nibbled on the muffin. It was obvious that the clerk was in no hurry to assist the woman. He lightly brushed off crumbs that had fallen on his keyboard and then logged onto the reservation system almost as if his hands were stuck to the keys. The woman, after having stood there for an inordinate amount of time, had finally reached her wits end.

Minutes later, the clerk, now gazing at the computer screen as if he were in a hypnotic trance, began to type on the keyboard with his index fingers. As this psychological tug-of-war played out, several passengers waiting in line had begun to show signs of impatience; some had moved to another line in hopes of avoiding any further delays.

"Nope. Ain't nothin' 'vailable till tomorrow night at 9:45," the clerk said, a look of subtle satisfaction etched across his face.

"Are you serious? That's unacceptable," she exclaimed.

"That's the way it is, Ma'am…ain't nothin' I can do 'bout it," he said. "Now, if you don't mind, I gotta assist the other customers. They been waitin' in line fo' a long time."

Not one to take no for an answer, the woman stepped aside, removed a cell phone from her purse, punched up the

C.F.C. website and looked at the online reservation information. She returned to the ticket window, and said, "Sir, I find it odd that, according to your website, there are plenty of spaces available on the nine and eleven o'clock ferries."

Another customer chimed in.

"Did I hear you say that you were able to access the C.F.C. reservation system online? Why, just yesterday, I wasted five hours attempting to book a reservation. And each time, the website had frozen, and then it booted me out. It's unbelievable! I felt so disgusted; I decided to drive down from Boston, only to witness the B.S. you're going through. What a joke. In my opinion, the whole damn bunch of these do-nothing idiots ought to get fired," the man said.

A man standing near the back of the line had had enough of the bickering between the woman and the clerk.

"Hey! Lady! Why don't you just accept the fact that the boat is sold out; there aren't any reservations available. You're holding up the line; we're gonna miss the ferry!" he yelled.

The woman turned and glared at the man, then said, "Why don't you mind your own business!" Embarrassed and red-faced, the man cowered and quickly retreated back into the line.

She turned back to the clerk, and said, "What's your name?"

"Fred Almeida," he said, his face beet-red from having been caught in a bald-faced lie.

"Better yet, what's your supervisor's name? I'm going to file a formal complaint. You and I know that there are empty spaces on at least three ferries this morning. But, for some reason, you're acting like a jackass that's on an ego trip, and I'm not going to stand for it! You've messed with the wrong person, buster. Now, I'd like the name of your supervisor," she demanded.

The clerk quickly glanced at the computer screen again, and said, in a muted tone, "I see there's a space available on the nine o'clock ferry this morning. Wanna book it?"

"Yes," she said.

"That'll be $62.50, one way. You gonna need any passenger tickets?"

"No."

"Well, all righty, then. Here's your boarding pass for the car."

"Thanks," she said.

"No, I thank you! Have a nice day," he said.

"Have a nice day? It *was* a nice day before I had to deal with your arrogant attitude," she muttered under her breath as she walked briskly out of the building.

One hour later on the Vineyard, the crew of the ferry Islander had begun to load the vessel for the 10:00 a.m. trip to Woods Hole. Two C.F.C. employees were standing on the ramp that led to the freight deck. One was collecting tickets; the other was guiding vehicles on to the ferry. An elderly couple, in their mid-to-late seventies, sat in a 1977 charcoal-gray Oldsmobile Cutlass Supreme and waited to drive aboard.

Finally, the vehicles began to move. As they slowly crept forward, the elderly gentleman maneuvered the car on to the ramp and stopped to give his boarding pass to the C.F.C. employee. Suddenly, the car's engine stalled. The driver was cognizant of the fact that he was preventing the other vehicles from boarding and attempted to restart the car. It would not start. A loud, high-pitched squeal came from the starter motor as it struggled to crank the engine. But after several attempts, the car would not start.

Just then, a C.F.C. employee named Tim—a short, burly man with a rugged-looking face speckled with acne, baggy beige slacks, soiled blue shirt and disheveled brown, curly hair—approached the car to inquire as to what the problem was.

"Hey! What's going on here? Start the damn car, old man! What the hell's wrong with you?" Tim asked.

"I'm trying to start it," the man said, in a nervous tone.

Suddenly, a second C.F.C. employee, Mack, walked over and said, "Take it easy, Tim. Can't you see that he's *trying* to start the car?"

"Because of you, we're gonna be late!" Tim shouted as he pointed his finger at the driver, and then flapped his arms like a bird ready to take flight. "Hey! You stupid old geezer—didn't you hear me? I SAID…START THE DAMN CAR! I don't know why the registry of motor vehicles issues driver's licenses to senior citizens. At best, the majority of you are senile. And, at worst, you're headed either for the geriatric unit or the grave," Tim blurted out. Tim didn't seem concerned about how embarrassed he had made the man feel. Just as he was about to hurl more insults at the man, the engine sputtered and then started, causing a thick cloud of blue smoke to shoot out of the tail pipe.

The man, now flustered, inadvertently stomps on the gas pedal and causes the tires to screech as the car lurches forward and on to the freight deck, nearly crashing into the vehicle ahead of it.

"Dumb old bastard," Tim mumbled under his breath as he shook his head in disgust.

"You shouldn't have yelled at the old man like that," Mack said.

Tim peered at Mack, daggers in his eyes.

"Listen, Mack. We've got a job to do here. And if you, or anyone else has a problem with that, then so be it. Frankly, I don't give a damn. Besides, this job doesn't pay enough for us to take a bunch of bullshit from customers, let alone some old crow that should be an exhibit in a wax museum," Tim said, in a dismissive tone.

Mack, seemingly taken aback, said, "Well, Tim, if it weren't for the customers, your dumb ass wouldn't have a job."

With a mean scowl on his face, Tim glared at his coworker and flippantly gave him the finger.

In another incident on the Hyannis to Nantucket route, a young man, about thirty years old, happened to be standing outside on the upper deck of the ferry Ocean Spray. As he breathed in the briny salt air and enjoyed the panoramic view of the ocean and seagulls gliding effortlessly overhead, he lit a cigarette when a C.F.C. employee happened to stroll by.

"Hey! You! There's no smoking allowed on this ferry—inside or out," the C.F.C employee said. "Didn't you hear the announcement over the loudspeaker?"

"No," the man replied. "I must have been downstairs in my car at the time."

"Well, as you can see, that sign over there clearly states that smoking's not allowed," the C.F.C. employee said, pointing to a small, illegible sign posted on a wall seventy-five feet from where they were standing. The words were difficult to decipher not only due to distance and the size of the sign, but also because several of the letters were missing.

"What, that tiny sign over there that spells: N SM K NG?" the man asked.

"Yeah," the C.F.C. employee answered.

"It appears to be missing three vowels."

"So, what if it is? It still means the same damn thing. What's a vowel, anyway?"

This guy's an imbecile, the man thought.

"Never mind. Okay. I'll make it quick," he said as he took a long drag from the cigarette.

The C.F.C. employee, annoyed by the fact that his directive was being ignored, approaches the man, reaches over, and snatches the cigarette from his mouth. He then flicks it over the railing and into the water.

"Hey, what do you think you're doing, you jerk?" the man said.

"I told you that smoking's not allowed on this ferry."

"Who gave you the right to take my cigarette?"

"As long as you're aboard *this* ferry, buster, the Commonwealth Ferryboat Company gives me the right," he said.

The man looked at the C.F.C. employee, and said, "How would you like a kick in the ass?"

"And how would *you* like to be tossed overboard?" The C.F.C. employee countered.

The squabbling intensified, until finally, it reached fever pitch. They stood toe-to-toe and glared at each other, each waiting to see who would be first to make a move. Suddenly, the C.F.C. employee steps back, turns, and walks away. The young man, relieved that he hadn't gotten into a fistfight, plopped himself down in a deck chair, plucked another cigarette from the pack, and pondered the incredulousness of what had just happened. *That guy must be out of his mind,* he thought.

Chapter Seven

On the Monday after Memorial Day weekend, the ferry Sea Mist departed from the Vineyard on its way to Woods Hole. A family of three, a mother, father, and their young daughter and pet dog—a dusty brown, cocker spaniel—had made their way to the lunch counter on the upper deck of the vessel. Elated by the fact that they had found an empty booth next to a window, they quickly sat down to enjoy the sights as the vessel sailed across Vineyard Sound.

The daughter, a six-year-old bundle of energy with brown eyes and curly locks, not wanting to stay seated for very long, had begun to chase the dog—back and forth, up and down—to the consternation of other passengers. The child seemed to never grow tired enough to take a break from her rambunctious activity. The purser on board the vessel, sitting at a desk in a small office adjacent to the lunch counter, thumbing through paperwork, had received numerous complaints about a young child and a dog running amok. Now tasked with addressing the issue, he emerged from the office and made his way to where the family was seated.

The purser stood at the booth, and said to the mother, "Excuse me, Ma'am. I've received complaints about a little girl and a dog running around the room. Is it your daughter?"

"Yes," she said.

"Well, I'm going to have to ask you to keep her seated," he said.

"Why? What's the problem? My daughter isn't causing harm to anyone," she said.

"That might be true. But she could hurt herself if she were to fall or bump into someone or something. I'll have to ask you to please control your daughter. Also, pets aren't allowed in the lunch counter; it's against Board of Health regulations," he said.

Taken aback by the purser's stern rebuke, the mother said, "Listen, Bub, my daughter isn't harming anyone or doing anything wrong. She's just a child, playing with our dog. And the dog is on a leash, so, what's the problem?"

"I'm just following the rules, Ma'am."

"You know what you can do with your rules, don't you?" she said, in a curt tone.

The purser said, in a stern tone, "If you refuse to do as I have asked, then I'll have no choice but to report you to the captain. He'll then contact the State Police, and they'll be waiting at the dock when we arrive at Woods Hole."

The woman's husband, who up to that point had remained quiet, suddenly spoke. "Cindy, why don't you just do what the man asks? There's no need to make a scene," he said.

The woman turned and looked at her husband, a scowl on her face, and said, "Shut up, Walter! These C.F.C. employees think they're better than everyone else. Look at them, with their big egos, tattered uniforms, and disheveled appearance, not to mention those hideous neon-orange vests. What's more, some of them reek of body odor...they smell. And they have the audacity to act as if they're better? It's almost as if they're on a power trip. It's crazy. You know what I think? I think they're full of crap. I can't tell you how tired I am of their condescending attitude," she shouted, causing other passengers to sit up and take note of her boisterous verbal diatribe. The woman sprung from her seat, looked pitifully at her husband, then grabbed her daughter's hand and pulled on the dog's leash, and said, "Let's go downstairs to the car...I can't wait to get the hell off this goddam boat!"

Early Tuesday morning, May 30, John huddled in his office and pored over a stack of reports from Memorial Day weekend. He carefully scrutinized the gross receipts, making note of things that had gone smoothly at the boat line as well as those that had not.

What jumped out at him was the unusually high number of service-related customer complaints that had been filed by passengers. As general manager, John was responsible for investigating and resolving all complaints in a timely fashion.

By day's end, John felt completely overwhelmed. He couldn't wait to get home. He would have given anything to forget, even temporarily, the problems he had to contend with that day. But, to him, there were few things that a glass of champagne couldn't help put into perspective. After John had settled in at home, he sat down on the sofa in his living room and enjoyed a couple of flutes of bubbly. Soon, he had compartmentalized the day's challenges, effectively erasing them from his mind.

As the evening progressed, John began to feel leery of what the summer season would bring, most notably, the fate of the Islander. It was a reality that he continued to grapple with, a personal battle he had waged with himself. He found it difficult to come to terms with the fact that the summer of 2006 would be the ferry's last season on the Woods Hole–Martha's Vineyard route.

June, July, and August brought with it the usual challenges associated with managing the C.F.C. operation: reservation snafus; crowd control; maintenance problems; human resource issues; late, or cancelled trips. As expected, a barrage of customer complaints was received with the same frequency as the sun rises every morning. However, despite the plethora of issues, John felt that it was worth it because the summer season had been lucrative. And though revenues had increased, maintenance costs continued to plague the bottom line. The next C.F.C. Board meeting was scheduled for Tuesday, September 26th, and John wasn't looking forward to it.

On the day of the meeting, John boarded the Islander in Vineyard Haven for the 4:00 p.m. trip to Woods Hole. Though he knew he had to make the meeting by 5:00, he became anxious because high winds and rough seas had caused the ferry's departure time to be delayed. As a result, it left port thirty-seven minutes late, arriving at Woods Hole at 5:17. After John had disembarked, he sprinted to the administrative office building and ran up the stairs to the boardroom on the second floor. Before he entered the room, he stopped at the door to catch his breath. While standing there, he happened to overhear Mr. Grandly conversing with two board members. With his back facing the door, Mr. Grandly was unaware that John was within earshot.

"To be perfectly honest, I'm as giddy as a child on Christmas Eve. I can't wait for the new ferry to arrive. Then we can either sell or scrap that old rust-bucket Islander; she's like a giant vacuum cleaner that does nothing but suck up cash every month. It's such a waste," Mr. Grandly said. "After the new ferry begins service, I can assure you that you'll forget that that old, rusty, hunk o' junk Islander ever existed."

When John entered the room, one of the board members had attempted to signal to Mr. Grandly to tone it down. But it was too late. John had already heard the bulk of Mr. Grandly's disparaging remarks.

"Come in, John, come in," Mr. Grandly said as he waved to him to take a seat at the conference table, obviously caught off-guard.

"I apologize for being late. The ferry was delayed because of high winds," John said as he sat down.

"No need to apologize, John," said Mr. Grandly. "Okay, everyone's here, so, let's get the meeting underway. There are only two items on the agenda: the treasurer's report and the new ferry update. Mr. Cottonwood, would you be so kind as to oblige us and share this summer's quarterly financial report?" Mr. Grandly asked.

"Thank you, Chairman Grandly," Mr. Cottonwood said as he stood and quickly glanced around the room.

"Well, I'm happy to report that revenues for the last quarter have increased by twelve percent. However, operating costs have had an adverse effect on the increase. So much so, the C.F.C. is in the unenviable position of having to report a net loss for the quarter. In fact, the loss puts the C.F.C. twenty percent below the break-even point," the treasurer said.

"Do you happen to know what caused the loss, Mr. Cottonwood?" another board member asked.

"Maintenance," he answered. "Specifically, longer down times and higher expenses associated with replacing obsolete parts on the vessels. Also, within the past year, the price of diesel fuel has risen by a dollar fifty per gallon, he added."

"Mr. Cottonwood, what vessel or vessels are primarily responsible for the increase in maintenance expenses?" Mr. Grandly asked.

"According to my calculations, about sixty-six percent, or two-thirds of the increase can be attributed to the Islander. The next most expensive vessel is the freight barge, Serendipity," he said.

Mr. Grandly glanced at John, then said, "Thank you for sharing that information, Mr. Cottonwood. This is a perfect segue to the next agenda item...the new ferry." The chairman opened a black, leather-bound notebook sitting on the table and proceeded to give the board an update on the delivery of the new vessel.

"I'm pleased to announce that the delivery of the new ferry is right on schedule. She's due to arrive on New Year's Eve, December 31st. However, the vessel won't be brought into service until March. Soon after we take delivery, she'll undergo rigorous trial runs. Then, the Coast Guard will conduct a final inspection. When the vessel is deemed seaworthy, we'll continue to perform test runs for approximately two months. Not long after that, the Islander will be decommissioned and piloted to Groton, Connecticut. By then, we should know whether the New York Port Authority will purchase her or not. If not, then the Islander will be put up for auction or scrapped," Mr. Grandly said.

John cringed at the thought of the Islander being dismantled and sold as scrap metal.

"As you all know, this past June, we solicited the public for suggestions on what to name the new ferry. Well, the votes are in and have been tallied. I have the results in this envelope."

Mr. Grandly picks up the envelope and removes a single white sheet of paper. Everyone seemed to hold their breath as he glanced at the paper, ready to announce the name for the new vessel. He stands, looks around the room, and says, "The name, selected by an overwhelming majority is...Island Gold."

A low murmur swept through the room as the board members processed what they had just heard. And, based on their reaction, most seemed to think that the name was an appropriate one for the new ferry. However, one board member didn't seem so sure. Meanwhile, John sat stoic in his chair, a blank expression on his face. *Island Gold? What a lousy name for a ferry,* he thought.

"I'd like to thank all of you for your hard work. It was no small feat to acquire the new vessel. And it just goes to show what we're capable of when we work together as a team. I commend you for a job well done. I now hereby declare this meeting adjourned," Mr. Grandly said, with a strike of the gavel.

Work as a team? Yeah; right, John thought as he watched Mr. Grandly hasten out of the boardroom. The manner in which the chairman had left the room reminded him of disease-carrying cockroaches that scurry for cover when the lights suddenly come on. John felt disgusted. He knew that Mr. Grandly had undermined the procurement process and handed the ferry contract to the Mississippi Dry-Dock Company on a silver platter, all without having received one competitive bid. Just the thought of it made him want to yell out loud in protest.

No sooner than when Mr. Grandly had arrived back at his office, the telephone rang.

"Hello, Harold Grandly speaking, how can I help you?"

'Click' went the telephone, after which Mr. Grandly heard nothing but a dial tone. *Now, that was strange; perhaps it was just a wrong number,* he thought.

For the next several months—to keep his spirits high—John spent most of his time thinking of ways to cut costs and increase productivity at the Commonwealth Ferryboat Company.

October and November had gone by in a flash. Before he knew it, the Holidays had arrived. At this time of year, business slows to a snail's pace, and, with not much else going on, John counted the days to December 31st, the date the new ferry was scheduled to arrive. Though John had tried to maintain a game face, ultimately, he was unable to hide his true feelings.

Chapter Eight

At 5:00 a.m. on December 30th, John drove to the C.F.C. wharf in Vineyard Haven, only to find the new ferry, Island Gold, berthed in slip #2, next to the Islander. She had arrived one day earlier than expected. John felt a sense of awe by the size of the vessel; for she possessed three decks, was one-third longer than the Islander, and stood nearly twice as tall.

Later that morning, John and his management team met in his office before taking a tour aboard the new, state-of-the-art, double-ended ferry. A team of engineers from the Mississippi Dry-Dock Company were to lead the tour and answer any questions the C.F.C. management team might have.

At 10:30, the group boarded what appeared to be a monstrosity of a vessel, a behemoth, reminiscent of a miniature cruise ship. Island Gold came equipped with all the bells and whistles one would expect to find on a modern ferry: spacious design; two powerful diesel engines; contemporary accents; comfortable passenger seats; hydraulic doors and lifts; GPS tracking system; the latest in audio-video technology;

automated navigation; flat-screen TVs; Wi-Fi access; and the ability to perform a myriad of self-diagnostic tests.

Despite her size, Island Gold could travel 16 knots, faster than any other vessel in the fleet. It was widely believed that this larger, more efficient ferry would soon become the crown jewel of the Commonwealth Ferryboat Company.

Regardless of that fact, John de Souza was unimpressed. Perhaps it was because of his unflinching loyalty to the stalwart vessel, Islander. At times, while John putted around the office during the day, he would often say aloud, "They don't make 'em like they used to," referring to the lackluster quality of the ferries in the C.F.C. fleet.

Three months later, the Islander and Island Gold sat side by side in slips 1 and 2 at the Vineyard Haven wharf. In terms of optics, this was a big deal for the Commonwealth Ferryboat Company, for it marked the first day of service for Island Gold *and* the Islander's last trip to Woods Hole. Soon after having been decommissioned, the Islander would head to Groton, Connecticut.

The Vineyard Haven wharf had been decorated with red, white, and blue streamers and balloons. A huge American flag—mounted on the ladder of a fire truck and hoisted high above the ground—flapped aimlessly in the salty breeze. A makeshift wooden platform was rolled into position, and atop the platform sat a podium equipped with a microphone, low-wattage amplifier, and a pair of audio speakers.

Anchored in the harbor, just beyond the first breakwater, were two U.S. Coast Guard cutters waiting to escort the Islander on her final voyage across Vineyard Sound. Not far from the cutters, a fireboat stood ready to shoot bursts of water into the air, a salute to the Islander's 57 years of service to residents and visitors to Martha's Vineyard.

At approximately 9:42 a.m., a multitude of dignitaries and guests had begun to arrive for the decommissioning ceremony of the Islander and commissioning of the Island Gold, officially marking the transfer of service from the old vessel to the new. Also, more than two-hundred faithful fans of the Islander—many of whom had been life-long passengers—had purchased a ticket for the final voyage that, to them, represented the sad end of an era.

Among the passengers were two special guests: Joseph Silva—an eighty-year-old former chief engineer, and last surviving member of the Islander's original crew from 1950, and Danny Moore, who had served as Steward's Assistant aboard the ferry for five years. They were invited by the C.F.C. Board of Directors to attend the ceremony and to accompany the crew on the Islander's journey to Groton, Connecticut.

By eleven o'clock, the wharf teemed with people. Much of the crowd was comprised of misty-eyed spectators who had had fond memories of the Islander and were sorry to see her sail away to retirement. Also present were people who happened to show up with no idea of what was going on. Last, but not least, rounding out the attendees, was a throng of C.F.C. employees whose opinions of the spectacle had run the full gamut.

For lack of a formal announcement, Mr. Grandly unassumingly took to the podium. He stepped up to the microphone, adjusted it, and then surveyed the crowd. Minutes later, he began his impromptu speech.

"Good morning. It warms my heart to see so many of you here on this momentous occasion. The purpose of this event is to commemorate the dawn of a new era at the C.F.C., the passing of the torch, if you will."

He paused briefly, and then continued.

"As many of you know, the Motor Vessel Islander has been the longest-serving vessel in the C.F.C. fleet. But sadly, the time has come for her service to the island to end and be recorded forever in the annals of history."

However, in his heart, Mr. Grandly's true feelings were such that he couldn't wait for the old ferry to fade away into oblivion so that the baton could be passed to the new ferry, Island Gold.

"Our new vessel, Island Gold, will begin service to Martha's Vineyard at twelve noon today. That said, it is with a heavy heart that I formally announce the decommissioning of the Islander. Governor Patrick was kind enough to send a proclamation to mark this event, which will be on display at the C.F.C. administrative office in Woods Hole. I again thank you for being here, and I'm sure I speak for everyone in saying thanks to the Islander for fifty-seven years of faithful service to the Vineyard."

The crowd erupted in a wave of applause and cheers.

Immediately following Mr. Grandly's remarks, the Martha's Vineyard Regional High School Band performed a rendition of the song, *The Last Farewell,* by Roger Whitaker and the decommissioning ceremony had officially begun. Within minutes, the Islander was put out to pasture, retired like an old racehorse, no longer useful and destined for the glue factory. And Island Gold—brand spanking-new and glistening in the sunlight on that cool, crisp March morning—stood ready to begin service between Martha's Vineyard and the mainland.

At approximately 12:12 p.m., the Islander, filled with passengers and vehicles, departed Vineyard Haven wharf for the final time. As she slowly chugged out of the harbor, the two coast guard cutters and a helicopter joined the forlorn procession and escorted the aged ferry towards Cape Cod.

During the 45-minute trip, countless anecdotes were exchanged among passengers. Some stories evoked boisterous laughter, while others brought tears of melancholy. When the ferry had docked at Woods Hole, several people on board were reluctant to leave the vessel, for they knew this was the final farewell.

The last passengers to disembark from the ferry were an elderly couple—a wife and husband—who, in 1957, had boarded the Islander while on the way to their honeymoon after having exchanged marriage vows at an Episcopalian church not far from the wharf. As the woman walked out the door, but before going down the gangway, she turned and lightly brushed the outside wall of the vessel with her hand. It was similar to a mourner who had reached out to touch a casket as it was wheeled down the aisle of a church, headed to its final resting place at a cemetery.

An eerie quiet had fallen over the Islander after the last of the vehicles and passengers had disembarked. The freight deck was empty; it appeared desolate, barren. The only discernible sound was a low rumble coming from the vessel's diesel engines. The stout ferry, devoid of activity, bobbed gently up and down in the slip as it conformed to the ebb and flow of the ocean.

Chapter Nine

Captain Sinclair Swanson, First Mate Derek Benjamin, and Engineers, Francis Martin and Jackson Peluso, prepared for the trip to Groton, Connecticut—the final leg on the Islander's journey to retirement.

As ceremonial gesture to the oldest living survivor of the Islander's original crew, former engineer, Joseph Silva, was invited to accompany the current crew on the Islander's final trip. Steward's Assistant, Danny Moore, a portly, thick-boned young man with a round face, curly brown hair that fell just above his shoulders and who had worked on the ferry with Joseph for two summers, was also invited along. They sat quietly in the wheelhouse and watched the crew engage in a flurry of activity. No other crew members were on board.

Joseph, a lean, elderly man with a long, drawn face, full head of fluffy, snow-white hair, and long, slender fingers, felt elated to be aboard the Islander again after having retired over twenty-five years ago. In fact, the old ferry had once been like a second home to him. And though he was content to sit in the wheelhouse and absorb the sights and sounds of all that was going on around him, what he really wanted to do was go to the engine room; for it had been decades since he'd been there. Hot, cramped, and at times, unbearably loud, Joseph and his former shipmates used to jokingly refer to the engine room as the 'bowels' of the vessel.

The wisdom that Joseph had acquired throughout his long life should have given him pause about attempting the dangerous climb down the steep steel stairs to the engine room, particularly at his age and the fact that he was physically frail. But, being determined, he climbed down anyway.

When he entered the engine room, the poignant odor of diesel fuel wafted through his nostrils. Almost immediately, that familiar smell jogged his memory and had somehow wiped away the cobwebs that time had slowly spun in his aging brain. What had once been bits and pieces of fuzzy memories had been transformed into vivid recollections of experiences he had once had. Joseph quickly acclimated himself to his old surroundings. He recalled the countless hours he'd spent holed up in the confines of that noisy, claustrophobic space. Suddenly, feelings of nostalgia rained down on him like a waterfall, a deluge of liquid cascading downward to a crystal-clear pool, filled with fragments of the past that had been miraculously weaved back together. In his mind's eye, he saw his former coworkers—all of whom are now deceased. And he could still hear the timbre of their voices as they exchanged friendly banter and carried out orders given by the captain upstairs in the wheelhouse: "Ahead one-third power; idle; full reverse; ahead, three-quarter speed portside; full stop."

The brief time that Joseph spent in the engine room had stoked many fond memories. So much so, he felt compelled to go back upstairs and share a few of them with Captain Swanson,

First Mate Benjamin, and Danny Moore. But when he got back to the wheelhouse, he noticed that Danny wasn't there.

"Where's Danny?" Joseph asked.

"He went for a walk," the captain said.

While Joseph was downstairs in the engine room, Danny had left the wheelhouse and took a stroll on the upper deck. As he walked, he happened to notice that many items had been confiscated from the vessel: a bronze bell; several door handles; the black and gold 'ISLANDER' name plate; nautical maps and various posters that had once hung on the walls. *Passengers must have taken them for mementos,* he thought. Just as he was making his way back to the wheelhouse, he felt a slight nudge as the ferry pulled away from the dock. The final leg of the trip had begun.

Danny returned to the wheelhouse, only to find Captain Swanson and Joseph Silva exchanging stories about their experiences aboard the Islander. He sat down, mid-conversation, and listened.

"...Boy, that certainly was a harrowing trip," Joseph said. "I thought we'd never make it to the dock in one piece."

"You don't say. What happened?" Captain Swanson asked.

"If memory serves me correctly, it was overcast on a Saturday afternoon in July 1962; around midday. Yeah, that's it...it was exactly twelve noon. Prior to our departure, there had been talk of canceling the trip because a Nor'easter was making its way up the eastern seaboard. It was expected to travel over Block Island and toward Cape Cod. The captain, fully aware of what the Islander was capable of and what she wasn't, had to decide. After having pondered for several minutes, he decided to make the trip. Shortly thereafter, we left port.

"On the way to Woods Hole, a freak thunderstorm seemed to have appeared from out of nowhere; it was a fast mover. It was almost as if we'd run into a hurricane!"

"Is that so? What happened?" the captain asked.

"Well, the wind velocity rose fast; in fact, it began to howl. It had to have been blowing between forty and sixty knots, with gusts around seventy-six. Several inexperienced crew-members in the engine room were wide-eyed with fear as they attempted to keep their balance while pulling levers and manipulating power to the diesel engines with white knuckles as the vessel pitched back and forth. However, it didn't faze me in the least. But what struck me was how the Islander responded to the weather conditions and rough surf. I'm downstairs in the engine room the whole time, mind you; I couldn't see outside. But I could feel the effects of the storm as the ferry's hull lifted out of the water and then dropped like an elevator falling down a shaft, pitching and yawing atop what had to have been twenty-foot ocean swells. It felt as if we were riding a roller coaster."

"Joe's right. I remember that day," Danny said. "I was eighteen years old. The ferry was thrashed about. I could hardly climb the galley stairs after I'd delivered sandwiches to the crew. That was one of the scariest seafaring experiences of my life!"

Joseph added, "And up in the wheelhouse, the captain, first mate, and the navigator had to cling to objects that were bolted down. Otherwise, they might've been swept away by the wind, rain, waves that crashed over the deck and into the wheelhouse, causing them to slip and slide on the wet floor."

"That's amazing," the captain said.

Joseph continued. "Anyway, of all the things I remember most about the trip, it was the strange sound of the engines that caught my attention. Each time the ferry dipped, the propellers, exposed to open air, caused the engines to make a high-pitched, whining sound. And those waves...I could hear each one crash against the hull with a loud bang; it almost sounded like a gunshot."

"That must have been something," the captain said.

"Sure was. But, for some reason, I felt safe. It never got to a point where I actually feared for my life," Joseph said.

"You don't say? What happened after that?" the captain asked.

"As we made our final approach to the dock at Woods Hole—after having navigated past the two outer markers—the captain called for maximum power and steered the vessel toward the starboard side. I don't know how he did it, but it was nothing short of masterful. Somehow, he used the fore and aft engines and rudders to guide the ferry into the slip. I had learned later that we almost entered the slip broadside. The ocean swells caused the ferry to slam against the berthing dolphins before it could be secured to the dock. The workers on the dock could barely keep their balance in the gale-force winds and deluge of rain, slipping and falling each time they tried to take a step. It was unbelievable!"

"Did the ferry sustain any damage?"

"Six broken windows and only a few dents to the portside of the vessel and one set of the freight deck doors," Joseph said.

"That was some story," Captain Swanson said as he navigated the ferry past Block Island.

"Tell me, Captain Swanson, you must have had some exciting experiences during your tenure as the skipper of this vessel," Joseph said.

"I certainly have," the captain replied. "One morning, the Islander almost sank."

"Really?" Danny asked.

"Yes. Let me tell you about it," the captain said.

"Captain, two sailboats forty-five degrees off the starboard side," the first mate warned.

"Roger. Thanks, Derek," he said.

The captain reached up and yanked on a brass lever hanging from the ceiling of the wheelhouse and sounded the deep, throaty air-horn to warn the sailboats of the ferry's approach.

"Now, where was I?" the captain asked. "Ah, yes. Back in March of 1980, we had just departed Oak Bluffs on the 9:15 a.m. trip to Woods Hole. The vessel was berthed at Oak Bluffs because, at the time, the Vineyard Haven wharf was under construction. About three hundred yards beyond channel marker twenty-three, somehow, we had struck an uncharted boulder off East Chop. The impact ripped five holes in the Islander's hull, one of which was about five feet in diameter. As you can imagine, we began to take on water at a pretty fast clip. The crew did their best to pump out the water, but it was of no use. Water gushed in at a rate that was impossible to control.

"So, what'd you do?" Joseph asked.

"My first instinct was to turn the ferry around and head back to the dock. But then I realized that that would be impossible because the hydraulics that controlled the rudder had been damaged; there was no way to steer the vessel. So, I shut down the engines and dropped anchor just beyond the entrance to Oak Bluffs Harbor. In order to keep the ferry afloat, a U.S. Coast Guard cutter and two tugboats pulled alongside her and propped her up. If they hadn't done that, she would have sunk," he said.

"Why didn't they tow the vessel?" Danny asked.

"At the time, I didn't think that that was an option, particularly with a full load of vehicles and passengers on board. I was afraid that had we attempted that, she would have capsized."

"So, what'd you do?" Joseph asked again.

"We stayed put. But within thirty minutes, the weight of the water caused the ferry to list portside. That's when we decided to take the chance and tow the ferry to the Oak Bluffs wharf. Three tugboats carefully maneuvered us back to the dock. The Coast Guard placed an emergency call to a company that specialized in the repair of hulls, and they sent a team of engineering experts and two scuba divers to assist. After they had arrived, the divers dove under the vessel to check the extent of the damage. Soon afterwards, they began work to patch the holes. However, it took about five hours to complete the job."

"How long was the ferry docked at Oak Bluffs?" Danny asked.

"About a day and a half. What was frustrating about the whole ordeal was that, here we were, three hundred yards from the wharf and we couldn't get back to it on our own. And you talk about angry passengers? If any of them had had a gun, then, more than likely, I wouldn't be here today to talk about it. The following morning, after the holes had been patched, the ferry was towed to Fairhaven and placed in dry docking for major repairs," the captain said.

"How long was she in dry docking?"

"Six weeks."

"I guess the important thing was that the Islander didn't sink," Joseph said.

"True. Hey, Danny, what about you? I can't imagine you *not* having any memorable experiences during the time you were Steward's Assistant," the captain said.

Danny thought for a moment, and then said, "Though most of my time as an SA was spent aboard the steamship Nobska, during one trip on the Islander, a young man—who happened to be a friend of one of the crew members—attempted to throw former Defense Secretary, Randall MacNee off the Islander one night in September, 1972. If I remember correctly, the man was a local artist who had adamantly protested the Vietnam War. Rumor had it that he felt that that war was an unjust military incursion.

"How interesting," Captain Swanson said.

Danny continued. "When the young man happened to notice MacNee at the lunch counter, he kept a wary eye on him. Then, when MacNee stepped outside to the deck, the man followed close behind. Words were exchanged and a confrontation ensued. By the time help had arrived, MacNee was attempting to balance himself on the outer-edge of the deck, clinging to the railing, holding on for dear life. When the ferry arrived at Vineyard Haven, the police were waiting at the dock, ready to apprehend the alleged assailant. But during the confusion, the crew member must have led his friend to the stern of the vessel where he jumped off before the gangway was lowered. That had to have been what happened because the police searched the entire vessel and the man was nowhere to be found. After he had jumped ship, he seemed to have just vanished. To this day, as far as I know, he was never caught. I had heard later that MacNee refused to pursue the matter. I guess he just wanted to put the incident behind him," Danny said.

"That's an incredible story, Danny. Thinking back, I remember hearing about it, but had never met anyone who was on board when it happened," Captain Swanson said.

"Yeah; that was something," Danny said.

Captain, we'll be arriving at Groton in about an hour," First Mate, Derek Benjamin said.

"Thank you, Derek. Please call the shipyard and confirm our arrival. I want to make certain they're prepared to take delivery of the vessel as soon as we dock," the captain said.

"Roger," Ben said.

"Captain, have arrangements been made for our return trip?" Danny asked.

"Yes. We're flying back to Woods Hole in a helicopter, compliments of the U.S. Coast Guard. In fact, it's the same chopper that escorted us on the trip to Woods Hole. They'll be waiting for us at a heliport not far from the shipyard," Ben said.

"Now that's what I call service," Joseph said, with a wide grin.

"Joe, weren't you working on the Islander when she had to hunker down on Naushon Island during Hurricane Carol, in 1954?" Danny asked.

"As a matter of fact, yes, I was. The captain was fortunate to have found a sheltered cove. He navigated the vessel there to ride out the storm. In my thirty-seven years as chief engineer on the Islander, that's the only time I can remember being forced to take refuge. I suppose no vessel can withstand 105 mile-per-hour wind gusts; not even the Islander," Joseph said.

Before long, the Islander entered the mouth of the Thames River and chugged towards the shipyard in Groton. Captain

Swanson maneuvered the ferry to a berth at the far end of the dock. After securing the vessel, the captain spooled down the engines before shutting them off.

The crew gathered a stack of documents and various other personal effects and then disembarked the ferry for the final time. The captain and his crew, with Joseph and Danny following closely behind, stopped and turned to catch one last glimpse of the old vessel. In what looked like an exercise in solemnity, they made their way to a heliport about a quarter mile down the road where they would board a U.S. Coast Guard helicopter for the flight back to Woods Hole. While walking, they noticed a foul metallic odor wafting in the air, reminiscent of something you'd smell at a steel mill or Sulphur factory. *Perhaps the odor was coming from the naval base, two miles up the river*, Captain Simpson thought to himself.

They boarded the helicopter, and within minutes, it lifted off the ground. In deference to how the pilot imagined his passengers felt at that moment, he flew the chopper several hundred feet in the air and briefly hovered above the Islander. From that vantage point, not only were decades of wear and tear on the old ferry clearly visible—faded and chipped paint, rust spots dotting the steel hull and doors at both ends of the vessel, dents in her side—it was obvious that she had been poorly maintained. The C.F.C. had adopted a band-aide approach to maintaining the ferry, doing only what was necessary to keep the old vessel afloat. Even if she had been properly maintained, there was no mistaking that the ferry's utility had long since been depleted; her service life was at its end. It was easy to see the extent of the vessel's deterioration; it was long past the time for her retirement.

As the helicopter flew up and away from the shipyard, everyone on board watched the somber image of the Islander grow smaller and smaller, until it was reduced to a tiny, white speck that seemed to disappear into the abyss of the murky Thames River. During the flight to Woods Hole, neither the crew of the Islander, nor Joseph or Danny, had much to say. Perhaps it was because they were immersed in the privacy of their own thoughts, coming to terms with the reality that the Islander was now nothing more than a compilation of fond memories to be cherished for years to come.

After having arrived back at Woods Hole, Captain Swanson and Derek Benjamin thanked Joseph and Danny for accompanying them on the trip. The captain and first mate said their goodbyes and began walking towards the ticket office. Suddenly, they were approached by C.F.C. Dock Manager, Terry Bloom.

"Captain Swanson! Captain Swanson," Terry yelled as he trotted towards the two men. He was huffing and puffing, struggling to catch his breath, almost as if he were having an anxiety attack. "Captain, I need to speak with you."

"Hello Terry," the captain said. "What's going on?"

"I was hoping you could tell me," Terry said.

"Tell you what?"

"I know this is going to sound bizarre, but, about an hour ago, I was on the dock inspecting the repair work that was being performed on the berthing dolphins, when, out of nowhere, the Islander sailed past and headed south towards Martha's Vineyard."

"What?" the captain replied.

"I'm telling you the truth," Terry implored.

"That's impossible," the captain said.

"When did that happen?" First Mate Derek Benjamin asked.

"About an hour ago."

"There's no way that that could have happened, Terry. This morning, we navigated the Islander to Thames Shipyard, in Groton Connecticut. In fact, a U.S. Coast Guard helicopter dropped us off at Otis Air National Guard base not more than thirty minutes ago," the captain said.

"I know it sounds crazy, but I'm telling you both, it *was* the Islander," Terry said.

The three men glanced at each other, expressions of dismay on their faces, and then went about their business. Terry returned to the dock, while Captain Swanson and Derek Benjamin walked in to the ticket office.

Chapter Ten

The Islander sat at Thames Shipyard for the better part of a year. Shortly thereafter, the C.F.C. entered into a Purchase and Sales agreement with the New York Port Authority, who had planned to use the ferry to shuttle passengers between Manhattan and Staten Island. Purchase price: five-hundred thousand dollars—as is.

One month later, Harold Grandly was in his office, mulling over the agenda for the next C.F.C. board meeting, when the telephone rang.

"Yes, Jane?"

"Mr. Grandly, I have a Mr. Theodore Spencer from the New York Port Authority on the line," she said.

"Please put the call through, Jane."

"Yes, sir," she replied.

"Good morning, Mr. Spencer. What a pleasant surprise it is to hear from you. How are things going with the refurbishment of the Islander?" Mr. Grandly asked.

"Funny you should ask—we have a problem, and that's what I'm calling about, Mr. Grandly."

"Oh? What seems to be the problem?"

"Let me be frank with you, Mr. Grandly. As you know, the New York Port Authority had every intention of using the Islander on the Manhattan to Staten Island run.

"Yes, I'm aware of that, Mr. Spencer."

"Well, two weeks after we had taken possession of the vessel, a subsequent inspection revealed fatal structural problems that were not discovered initially. What's more, in order for the vessel to pass the stringent Coast Guard inspection, six million dollars' worth of repairs would be needed, an investment the New York Port Authority is loathed to make for an old ferry that's literally rotting away at the seams.

"I'm sorry to hear this news, Mr. Spencer. But, I must remind you that, according to the terms of the sales agreement, the ferry was sold 'as is'," Grandly said.

"Are you saying that the C.F.C. is unwilling to negotiate even a partial reimbursement?" Mr. Spencer asked.

"I'm sorry, but no."

"What do you expect us to do with the vessel?"

"You could always auction her off for scrap metal and write the loss off as a business expense," Grandly said.

"Five-hundred thousand dollars down the drain! Thanks for nothing."

"This isn't personal, Mr. Spencer; it's just business."

"Yeah—monkey-business," he retorted, before slamming the telephone down on the cradle.

Chapter Eleven

When The New York Port Authority's plan to refurbish the ferry was scuttled, the Islander sat at Staten Island for another three years before it was finally auctioned off to a New Jersey scrap-iron dealer who offered a measly twenty-six thousand dollars for the vessel. Much to the dealer's surprise, the offer was accepted. Seven months later, the Islander was finally towed to Port Newark, New Jersey and scheduled for dismantling.

When John had learned of the Islander's fate, it affected him deeply. He had hoped that the ferry could somehow be saved by converting it into a floating restaurant, or a maritime museum. John was invited to New Jersey to witness the dismantling, but he declined because he couldn't bear to see his favorite ferryboat ripped apart and sold for scrap.

The demolition commenced on a Wednesday and took only a day to complete. After the fixtures had been removed, a huge crane—equipped with an iron ball and what resembled a giant pair of scissors—tore into the ferry, effectively ripping it to shreds. Strips of sheet metal were peeled away from the Islander's frame like the skin on an onion. In the end, all that was left of the vessel was its rusty hull, stripped down to a skeletal carcass that lay abandoned at the shoreline, sitting halfway in the water.

On the evening of the Islander's dismantling, John and Elisa, after having finished their dinner, sat at the kitchen table, each with a cup of coffee before them. Elisa got up from her chair and began to clear away the dishes, while John, in an attempt to distract himself from the somber events of the day, buried his head in the *Vineyard Gazette* newspaper.

"John, this Friday is Good Friday," Elisa said.

"Yes, Elisa. I know that," he said.

"I'd like to attend the church service after work. Do want to come with me?"

John lowered the newspaper, looked at his wife, and said, "Don't I make it a point to go with you every year?"

"Not every year," she said, with a smirk. "You didn't attend last year because you had to work."

"That's correct, Elisa. I didn't make it to the service last year. But it wasn't my fault; I had to cover for a manager who had called-in sick," he said.

"All too often, John, you go out of your way for the C.F.C. I'm sure they're overjoyed to have you as an employee because you seem to have been forged out of the company mold!" she said.

"Please, Elisa, give me a break, won't you? You know that that's part of the job," he implored as he bowed his head and turned his attention back to the newspaper.

Throughout her childhood, Elisa's family celebrated Easter religiously. They prepared Easter baskets the evening before and faithfully attended church services on Easter morning. It was a tradition that Elisa had observed all through life, and this year was no exception.

On Thursday morning, at the Vineyard Haven terminal, John peeked out his office window and looked towards the dock, only to see a large crowd milling around as they waited to board the new ferry, Island Gold. More than fifty vehicles, which should have been aboard the vessel, were lined up behind one another in the staging area next to the parking lot.

Three C.F.C. employees standing on the freight deck of the vessel, seemed to be struggling to open the hydraulic doors. John glances at his watch—10:26 a.m. *There must be something wrong; the ferry should have left the dock twenty-six minutes ago*, he thought.

Curious to see what the delay was, John made his way to the door. But before he reached it, the telephone rang. He turned, walked back to his desk and picked up the handset.

"Hello?" he said.

"John, this is Mack. You better git down here right away... we got a problem," he said.

"What is it?"

"It be the new ferry. Somethin's wrong wit' one of the freight deck doors; it's stuck half-open. It won't budge."

"What? The door isn't working?" John asked in disbelief.

"Sure 'nuff. And the passengers are gettin' antsy. Whudda ya want us ta do?"

"I'll be right down," John said.

John raced down the stairs, only to find that tempers had already begun to flare inside the ticket office. Customers were arguing with C.F.C. employees, demanding answers to questions to which they had none. John had managed to snake his way through what appeared to be a mob-scene and slip out a side door. When he reached the ramp, the exasperated crew member turned toward him—discombobulated and red-faced—and said, "This vessel's a piece a shit! This NEVER woulda happened on the Islander!"

"Is there a manual override for the doors?" John asked.

"Yeah, there is. But that's not workin' either," Mack said.

"I can't believe this is happening," John muttered under his breath.

John dashed back to his office and placed a telephone call to the C.F.C. Communications Center in Woods Hole. Not knowing what to do, he requested that two freight barges be sent to Vineyard Haven. One barge would replace the delayed trip caused by the mechanical problems on the new ferry, and the other to help alleviate the backlog of passengers and vehicles that seemed to grow larger by the minute.

At that point, the C.F.C. added more ferry trips to the schedule. And by the end of the day, operations had returned somewhat to normal. However, in order to address the mechanical problems that had sidelined the ferry, Island Gold, John decided to take her out of service. Fortunately, a freight barge happened to be sitting at Woods Hole which could be used to cover Island Gold's remaining trips.

That evening, three mechanics from the Mississippi Dry-Dock company worked to repair the malfunctioning hydraulic door on the new ferry. But, while doing so, they discovered another problem: both the primary and backup generators had failed. Neither would convert mechanical energy to electric energy.

"How long will it take to repair the generators?" John asked the mechanic in a concerned tone.

The mechanic looked at John, a matter-of-fact expression on his face, and said, "They can't be repaired. The motors on both generators are burned out. From the looks of it, they're useless. There's no repairing these suckers…they've got to be replaced."

"Okay. So, how long will that take?"

"I can't say for sure. These generators are unique, a prototype; brand new design. Unfortunately, we don't have spares on hand. The only option is to have two new generators shipped here from Louisiana," he said.

"Are you serious? You must have *some* idea of how long it'll take. What, a day? Two days?" John asked, in a curt tone.

The mechanic turns to John, and says, "If the generators are shipped overnight and they arrive by noon tomorrow, then we can install them in about six to eight hours. In that case, I'd guess the vessel should be ready to go tomorrow afternoon between four and six o'clock."

John performed a quick calculation in his head, attempting to figure out the number of trips he'd have to cover as a result of Island Gold's mechanical problems. It wasn't going to be easy. At a minimum, he'd have to use a freight barge from Woods Hole *and* remove another vessel from the Nantucket route and reassign it to the Martha's Vineyard route.

Inevitably, John's worst fears had materialized; the domino effect was in full force. None of the vessels had departed on time, and, it seemed as if disarray had surreptitiously infiltrated the C.F.C. terminals at Woods Hole, Oak Bluffs, and Vineyard Haven. What's more, substantial delays had been reported on the Nantucket route. To help alleviate the backlog of vehicle traffic, standby service was suspended at all three ports. And, if you didn't have a reservation for your vehicle, you could bet you weren't going anywhere soon. In order to keep the tempers of disgruntled customers from escalating into fistfights, State Police officers were stationed at each C.F.C. terminal.

No doubt this was one of the worst days of John's twelve-year career at the C.F.C. After the last ferry of the evening had departed, John—physically and emotionally exhausted—sat at his desk and stared blankly at the wall. He couldn't fully comprehend the extent of the issues he had dealt with that day, all attributable to the mechanical failure of the new ferry, Island Gold.

John had spent all of Friday attempting to rectify the scheduling problems caused by Island Gold's unexpected breakdown. And, by late afternoon, the situation had not gotten any better. But in order to keep his promise to accompany Elisa to Good Friday church services, John reluctantly left the office at 4:30 p.m. and made his way home. There was no way he was going to miss the church service two years in a row.

Early Saturday morning, John headed for the office to pick up where he had left off the day before. At 10:33 that evening, still holed up at the office, John attempted to put together an impromptu ferry schedule for the following day. Realizing he hadn't eaten anything since breakfast, he trudged to the employee lunchroom and bought a steak and cheese sandwich out of a vending machine, only to find that the expiration date written on the cellophane wrapper had long since passed. Not to be dissuaded, he let out a sigh and walked over to the microwave oven to heat the sandwich. As luck would have it, the microwave was inoperative. At that point, his hunger pangs forced him to eat the cold sandwich.

John returned to his desk and, once again, thought about the problems he had dealt with that day. It was one for the record books. Chaos had taken center stage, all because the new ferry had failed to live up to the hype. In a moment of frustration, John snatches the telephone off the desk and dials Chairman Grandly's number.

After several rings, John heard the phone go 'click', but it sounded as if no one was on the other end of the line.

"Hello? Mr. Grandly?"

"Yes, this is Grandly. John? Is that you?" he asked, in a scratchy voice.

"Yes. I thought I heard the phone pick up, but I didn't hear you say anything," John said.

"Well, um—lately, I've been receiving prank calls and thought this was another one. Do you realize it's almost midnight? Why are you calling at this hour? Is there an emergency of some sort?"

"Well, yes; sort of," John said.

"What is it?"

"I'm very concerned about what happened today. It's really bothering me, and I've got to get it off my chest."

"Can't it wait till morning?" Mr. Grandly asked.

"No."

"All right, John. What is it, specifically?"

"It's about your so-called, thirty-two-million-dollar wonder-boat, Island Gold."

"What about it?" Mr. Grandly asked.

"Haven't you heard?"

Grandly paused, and then said, "Heard what?"

"Well, she *really* shat the bed today," John said.

"What in the world are you talking about, John?"

"Your crowned jewel…she broke down and had to be taken out of service. I can't even begin to tell you about the scheduling nightmare it has caused."

"What's wrong with the ferry?" Mr. Grandly asked.

"One of the doors to the freight deck had become stuck. And soon after that, the primary and backup generators had failed. The mechanics had no choice but to special order two new generators and have them flown up from Louisiana," John said.

"That's not such a big deal, John. I'm sure you've dealt with more serious problems than that. Besides, you're the general manager—handling things of this nature is *your* responsibility; it's part of the job."

"Mr. Grandly, you know as well as I that this would never have happened on the Islander."

"Oh, please spare me, John. There you go again, spouting off about the Islander. Why can't you accept the fact that that old rust bucket is gone? She was nothing but a drain on the C.F.C.'s bottom line. Get over it, man. It's high time you moved on," he said.

Within a millisecond, John had become angry; he saw red. He couldn't help thinking about the events that led to the Islander's demise: the corrupt, back room deals; misrepresentation; manipulation of the bidding process; the blatant impropriety and lack of integrity by C.F.C. board members.

Unable to contain his emotions any longer, John said, "I know all about the shenanigans that occurred to acquire the new ferry. And from what I can tell, it seems as though the bidding process was rigged from the start."

"What are you implying, John? Are you accusing the C.F.C. Board of Directors of engaging in underhanded tactics? The board acquired the new ferry in accordance with established procurement protocols. We followed the law to the letter. The entire process was handled by the book...and *that* you can be sure of!" Mr. Grandly said.

"Come now, Mr. Grandly. Why don't you wake up and smell the bullshit you're shoveling? I might not be the brightest bulb on the Christmas tree, but it sure seems as if you're working overtime to insult my intelligence. Your futile attempt to pull the wool over my eyes is a perfect example of that," John said.

"Pull the wool over your eyes? What makes you think I'm trying to do that?" Mr. Grandly retorted, in a defensive tone.

"Well, for starters, as far as the contract for the new ferry is concerned, there was no public solicitation for bids, at least not that I'm aware of. And correct me if I'm wrong, but I don't believe that the board ever submitted a formal request for proposals. If it had, then I would have at least heard about it. And I've heard nothing."

"John...John...John. You know damn well that the bidding process is confidential. No one, AND I MEAN, NO ONE, other than members of the board, is privy to what bids have been received for the contract and from whom."

"Exactly," John said.

"Listen, John. I can understand how the fate of the Islander has been disconcerting to you. I know how fond you were of her. But she's gone now, and I'd suggest you do whatever's necessary to get over it and move on. The Island Gold is here, and she's here to stay," Grandly said.

In response to Mr. Grandly's condescending tone, John felt tempted to reveal what he knew as fact, but then thought about the ramifications of doing so. Not only might he be in danger of losing his job, but his brother-in-law, Ralph, could also lose his. What's more, John was cognizant of the irreparable harm it could do to his marriage. And he couldn't bear the thought of hurting his wife if she were to learn that he had caused Ralph to be fired. Taking that risk wasn't worth it, so, once again, he decided to remain mum.

"John, I understand how you feel. But, if you find it too difficult to deal with, then perhaps it might be best for you to consider pursuing another line of work," Grandly said.

After listening to Mr. Grandly's diatribe, John's blood pressure had risen to a point where he felt as if steam was about to shoot out of his ears. His disdain for Mr. Grandly had only grown stronger because he believed that he'd crossed a red line; he felt true antipathy towards him.

During the conversation with Mr. Grandly, John had noticed that he had been gripping the telephone so tight; his hand had begun to hurt. And when he switched the phone to the opposite hand, he was surprised by how stiff it felt, not to mention that it had turned a deep purplish-red, as if his hand had been bruised. Somehow, John managed to calm down, and said, "That won't be necessary, Mr. Grandly. I think I just need a good night's sleep. I'm sure I'll feel better in the morning."

"That's the spirit, John. If I were you, I wouldn't worry about this. Everything's going to be just fine. Good night, John."

"Good night," he said.*If only I felt the same as you,* John thought to himself as he hung up the telephone.

Shortly after Mr. Grandly had gotten back into bed and turned off the light, the telephone rang again. He quickly jumped up again and answered it.

"Hello, John?" he asked.

A muffled voice on the other end, barely audible, said, "No, Mr. Grandly, this isn't John. You don't know me. But you can bet that I know you. I also happen to know that you were responsible for rigging the procurement process for that over-priced passenger ferry, you scoundrel. Corrupt weasels like you are nothing but yellow cowards who ought to be swimming with the fishes. But, then again, death is too good a punishment for you. Listen carefully, you lyin', cheatin' punk. I promise you this...you won't get away with it, you scumbag."

"Hello? Hello? Who is this?" asked Mr. Grandly.

'Click' went the telephone.

It was just before midnight when John left the office and headed for home. While driving, he felt deeply disturbed and wondered whether he should consider Mr. Grandly's suggestion to resign from the C.F.C. After all, he did have his pride. But what else could he do for work? Management positions that pay a living wage on the Vineyard are in short supply, if not non-existent. And any other employment opportunity would most likely be off island. At best, he'd have to commute to Cape Cod, and, at worst, he'd be forced to travel to Boston. He shuddered at the thought.

When John arrived at home, he crept into the house so as not to disturb Elisa, who was upstairs in bed, asleep. He went into the kitchen and made a smoked turkey sandwich on whole wheat bread with lettuce, tomato, a slice of Cheddar cheese, and spicy Dijon mustard. Next, he grabbed hold of a blue and white cellophane bag of Cape Cod potato chips—the logo of a lighthouse printed on the wrapper—from the cupboard. John reached into the bag, grabbed a handful of chips, and piled them on a plate.

After wolfing down the sandwich and chips, he sat stoic at the table and began to think morbid thoughts, causing him to become angry and depressed, all while falling into the depths of helplessness and depression. Being a man of integrity, John found the corruption at the C.F.C. intolerable. He felt the need to calm his nerves by the only way he knew how. He grabbed a bottle of Dewar's Scotch and a shot-glass from the cupboard and made his way to the living room. After plopping himself down in the easy chair, he began to sip the Scotch. It wasn't long before he had drunk the whole bottle.

While leaning back in the chair, giddy from intoxication, John nodded off to sleep with the empty shot glass in his hand. Suddenly, he was awakened by the sound of the glass as it fell to the hardwood floor and rolled to a stop against the television console. Although John was awake, he wasn't cognizant. His fuzzy state of mind had somehow displaced the need for sleep. After having drunk himself into a stupor, he attempted to ward off the effects of a debilitating hangover. He looked at the coffee table, only to see what appeared to be an oversized Easter basket sitting on top. As John gazed at the basket, he noticed that it was lined with strands of fake green grass—similar to a bird's nest—and contained five hard-boiled eggs decorated in an assortment of colors and patterns; four chocolate bunnies; six miniature yellow chicks made of marshmallow; and a greeting card in a bright pink and purple envelope that Elisa had stood upright behind the basket. With no desire to go upstairs to bed, John decided to go to the office instead and get an early start to the workday.

Chapter Twelve

Easter Sunday, April 24. It had been three days since the Islander was dismantled and sold for scrap. On his way to the office, John found himself immersed in a thick fog that slowly drifted in from the east. As he continued toward the wharf in Vineyard Haven, he could hardly see the boats moored in the harbor. In fact, the flashing red beacon at the end of the breakwater was almost indistinguishable.

John glanced at his watch—3:47a.m. The intense throbbing in his head felt like a hammer hitting against an anvil, and only got stronger with each beat of his heart. He felt as if he had had a migraine headache. "That damned Scotch numbs the senses," he muttered aloud.

John drove down State Road through the fog and made a left turn at five corners. As he approached the Stop & Shop across the street from the ferry terminal, a large, mechanical bunny rabbit, standing upright in a display window while holding an Easter basket in its left paw, almost seemed to wave indiscriminately at him as he drove into the C.F.C. lot. He parked his car and headed for the ticket office. It was still early morning, not a soul was around. The only sounds he heard were that of crickets and various nocturnal creatures as they scurried about. And though there was barely a breeze, the fog seemed to drift effortlessly across the harbor and engulf the wharf in a thick, gray cloud that resembled white ashes from burned firewood. The entire waterfront, devoid of activity, seemed to exude a ghostly eeriness. Before John reached the ticket office, he turned and looked back at the dock. And what he saw stopped him dead in his tracks.

A vessel sat berthed in slip number one, next to the passenger ferry, Sea Mist. Though obscured by the fog, it resembled the Islander. At first glance, John thought it *was* the old ferry, but he knew that that was impossible because she had been destroyed three days earlier.

John dismissed what he thought he saw and simply attributed it to the Scotch he had drunk. *I must be hallucinating,* he thought.

While standing at the entrance to the ticket office, John rubbed his eyes with both hands. He paused, and then looked at the dock again, only to see what appeared to be the Islander. At first, he felt perplexed. He thought his eyes were playing tricks on him. Though he felt apprehensive, his curiosity compelled him to approach the vessel.

Still in disbelief, John walked down the ramp and peered through the open doors to the freight deck. There was no mistaking it was the Islander. Though empty inside, John could hear the familiar rumble of the vessel's diesel engines; it sounded like the low, guttural growl of a purring kitten, amplified a thousand-fold.

"I must have lost my mind," John said to himself as he turned and walked back to the office. When he got inside, he sat down at his desk, but then got up again and walked over to the window. He was hesitant to look outside for fear of confirming that he had, indeed, gone insane. But he couldn't resist temptation. He glanced out the window, hoping that his bout of delusion was only temporary and would soon pass.

It did not.

By 4:45 a.m., a bright orange glow from the sun appeared on the horizon. And soon, it began to burn off the fog that had settled over the area earlier that morning. Eager to confirm whether he had gone mad, or not, John counted down the minutes until the first C.F.C. employees arrived at work. The crew on the passenger ferry, Sea Mist, was always the first to arrive at the dock because they had to prepare for the 6:00 a.m. trip to Woods Hole.

John remained in his office while keeping a wary eye out for the crew. Astonished by what appeared to be an exact replica of the Islander, he couldn't stop staring at the ferry.

To look at it, the vessel appeared to be in pristine condition, brand-spanking new. In fact, it looked exactly like the Islander did on her first day of service in May 1950. Her outer skin, forged from sheet metal and painted bright white, had a long, narrow horizontal black stripe that framed the windows on either side of the vessel. It ran the entire length, ending at a point just before the freight deck doors. Her hull—constructed from surplus WWII submarine steel—was a glossy black and reflected the water underneath as shallow waves gently lapped against the stout ferryboat. Conspicuously inscribed on her hull, in white block letters: ISLANDER, Woods Hole.

"This is crazy," John uttered aloud.

At 5:15 a.m., four crew members arrived at the dock, only to be taken aback when they saw the Islander moored in the adjacent slip.

"What the...what the hell is this?" one of the crew members asked.

"It looks like the Islander," another said.

"But that's impossible! She was scrapped earlier this week! Or, was she?" a third crew member said.

"Do you think the C.F.C. had had the Islander refurbished and didn't notify anyone?" the fourth crew member inquired.

"No way. And even if that were the case, it would've taken months or years to accomplish that task. "Either someone's playing an elaborate trick on us, or, we've all gone nuts," Captain Simpson said.

When John saw the crew members standing on the dock, he raced down the stairs to join them. By then, more C.F.C. employees had arrived, and their reaction was similar to the others.

"John! What's going on here?" one of the crew members asked.

"I have no idea," John replied.

For the next several minutes, all they could do was stand there and gawk at something that was an impossible anomaly.

"What do you suggest we do, John?" Captain Simpson asked.

"I'm going back inside to make a telephone call to the board chairman, Mr. Grandly. In the meantime, I'd suggest you and your crew prepare for the 6:00 a.m. trip," he said.

"Yes, sir. All right, everyone, let's get aboard and get ready," he said to his crew.

The crew slowly made its way onto the ferry, Sea Mist. They were astounded by the presence of what could only be described as an aberration of the now defunct motor vessel, Islander.

No sooner than John had gotten back to his office, the telephone rang.

"Hello?" he said.

"John, you need to get back down here *right away.* If you think seeing the Islander again was something, you're not going to believe this," Captain Simpson said.

"I'll be right there," John said.

John glanced at the clock—5:42 a.m. Though confused, he dashed from his office and made his way back down the stairs. When he arrived at slip number one, he was shocked to see cars being guided on to the Islander by three men he had never seen before. The men were dressed in vintage C.F.C. uniforms: navy blue slacks, light blue, long-sleeved shirts, a round C.F.C. patch with bright red letters stitched above the left-hand pocket, and bulky, beige work boots.

As the cars inched onto the ramp, drivers stopped only briefly to hand their tickets to a tall, thin, older gentleman who appeared well-groomed. His complexion was pale white, and he had silver-gray hair and a bushy mustache shaped like motorcycle handlebars. After the drivers had surrendered their tickets, they maneuvered their vehicles onto the vessel. John approaches the gentleman collecting tickets, and says, "Excuse me, but what do you think you're doing? You can't do thi—"

"I'm sorry, sir, but we're loading the ferry. It's dangerous for you to be on the ramp now. You could get hurt, and we wouldn't want that to happen," the man said with a calm voice and warm smile, seemingly devoid of any aggression whatsoever.

"Who are you? And where did you come from?" John asked.

The man nodded at John and smiled, almost as if he were looking right though him. Then, he turned and resumed the task of collecting tickets and waving vehicles aboard. As each vehicle inched down the ramp, the man greeted the driver with the utmost courtesy. He politely asked for their tickets before two coworkers inside the vessel directed the vehicles to a parking space. After the last vehicle had boarded, the ferry prepared to leave port.

"Good morning, sir. Welcome aboard the Islander. We hope you have a pleasant trip and look forward to seeing you again soon," the crew member said to a driver who had stepped out of his car.

John, after having vehemently expressed his displeasure with what was happening, stood impotently on the ramp, flabbergasted by his inability to intervene. He watched the elderly crew member saunter onto the freight deck while two of his coworkers unhooked the fasteners to free the ferry from the ramp. A third coworker opened the door to a small metal box affixed to the wall, grabbed hold of a telephone inside, and dialed the number to the wheelhouse. "Captain, the freight deck is secure," he said.

Suddenly, three short blasts from the ferry's deep, throaty air-horn sounded, and the first of two heavy steel doors to the freight deck was pushed closed by three crew members. The diesel engines roared, and the propellers at the stern of the vessel rotated and caused the stout ferryboat to push away from the dock and out of the slip. Just as the Islander reached the breakwater, the second door closed with a loud *bang*.

Minutes later, a scratchy-sounding radio transmission had arrived at the communications center in Woods Hole. The quality of the transmission sounded archaic, as if outdated radio equipment were being used to send it.

"Motor Vessel Islander departing Vineyard Haven...6:02 a.m...Over."

The dispatcher on duty, amused by what he thought he had heard, responded, "Ferry Islander? Did you say, ferry Islander...Over?"

"Roger," the man answered.

"To whom am I speaking?" the dispatcher asked.

"This is Captain Sigmund Black," he said.

"Captain Sigmund Black? We have no one by that name employed at the C.F.C...Over."

"I repeat—this is Captain Black on the Motor Vessel Islander. We're due to arrive at Woods Hole at 06:30 hours. Please confirm...Over."

"Okay, Captain Black. Or, should I say Captain Simpson on the ferry, Sea Mist? Fellas, I get it. But it's kind of early in the morning to be engaging in practical jokes, isn't it?"

There was no response.

"Ferry Islander, though you're not due to arrive until six-forty-five, you're confirmed for a 6:30 arrival at Woods Hole, as requested...Over."

"Roger," the captain said.

I can't imagine what's gotten into Captain Simpson, the dispatcher thought.

As John was walking back to the ticket office, he heard his name being called from a distance. Captain Simpson ran up to him, and in a winded voice, said, "Sea Mist has no electrical power; it seems as if she's dead in the water."

"What do you mean she's dead in the water?" John asked.

"I don't understand it, but for some reason, there's no electrical power aboard the ferry. We were about to load the vessel for the six o'clock trip, when suddenly, everything went dead. I've placed a call to the electrical contractor, and they're sending over a technician to diagnose the problem," the captain said.

"Captain Simpson, did you happen to see what I saw at the dock?"

"Are you talking about the Islander?"

"Yes."

"Of course, I did. And now, *she's* making the 6:00 a.m. trip to Woods Hole, the one we were supposed to have made. What's more, she's carrying a full load of vehicles and passengers," Captain Simpson said.

"This can't be happening," John said.

"That's exactly what I thought. But, apparently, *it is* happening," the captain said.

"Excuse me, captain, but I've got to get back to the office. I must attempt to get a handle on this situation," John said. "Please keep me abreast of any changes in the status of your vessel."

"Will do," the captain said.

John watched from his office window as the Islander rounded West Chop and disappeared. He picked up the telephone and dialed the C.F.C. office in Woods Hole.

"Good morning. Commonwealth Ferryboat Company, Becky speaking; how may I help you?"

"Yes, Becky. This is John de Souza on the Vineyard. Is Bob Cunningham available? I must speak with him right away."

"Oh, hello, Mr. de Souza. Yes, please hold. I'll transfer your call."

"Thanks," he said.

She transferred the call, and Bob picked up the phone on the first ring.

"This is Bob Cunningham speaking," he said.

"Bob? John de Souza here. Listen, you're not going to believe what I'm about to tell you, but you must. This is *not* a joke!"

"Okay, John. What is it?"

"When I arrived to work this morning, I saw the Islander berthed in slip number one."

"The Islander," Bob said, in a sarcastic tone.

"That's correct...the Islander," John said.

"John, are you drunk or high on something, or just pulling my leg?"

"Neither. I'm telling you God's truth. It was the Islander. She's come back!"

"John, we both know that that's impossible. The Islander was scrapped three days ago. What's more, I have a stack of pictures on my desk that were taken during the demolition. In fact, I'm looking at them as we speak," Bob said.

"I know it sounds crazy, Bob. But it's true."

There was a loud knock on John's office door.

"Hold on, Bob." He lowered the phone and covered the mouthpiece with his hand. "Come in, the door's unlocked," he said.

Captain Simpson opened the door just wide enough to stick his head inside, and said, "John, I wanted to let you know that power has been restored on the Sea Mist."

"Please come in, captain. I have Bob Cunningham from the Woods Hole office on the phone. Bob, I'm putting you on speakerphone," John said.

"Hello, Bob? Can you hear me?"

"Yes, John. I can hear you," he said.

"Bob, I have Captain Simpson, skipper of the ferry, Sea Mist, here with me. He can verify what I'm telling you about the Islander," John said.

John waved to the captain to come closer, and then, pointing at the telephone, he motioned for him to speak.

"Mr. Cunningham, what Mr. de Souza says is true. The Islander is, in fact, on its way to Woods hole with a full load of vehicles and passengers," the captain said.

"Is there something in the air or water on the Vineyard that's affected both of you? What you're saying is preposterous, never mind it being beyond the realm of possibility."

John and Captain Simpson looked at each other, dumbfounded, unsure of what to say.

"Does the C.F.C. Board Chairman, Mr. Grandly, know about this, John?" Bob asked.

"No. You're the first person I called," he said.

Silence.

"Bob?"

"Yes, I'm here," he said.

"Well, I guess you're gonna have to see it for yourself when she arrives," John said.

"What are you talking about?" he asked.

"The Islander."

"So, you're still tryin' to get me to buy into that crazy story, huh?"

"It's no crazy story; you'll see," John said.

"Gentlemen, must I remind you that April Fool's Day has come and gone? I suppose next you'll tell me that elephants can fly, or that dinosaurs are roaming the earth again."

"Go ahead and have your fun. I'd bet you won't be laughing at 6:45," John said.

"Okay, you guys. Just to show that I'm a good sport, I'll go along with your little charade. You claim the Islander left the Vineyard at six. So, that means she should arrive here at 6:45, or thirty minutes from now, correct?"

"Yes, John answered."

"I'll tell you what. I'll be at the dock by six-thirty, just in case she happens to arrive early," Bob chuckled. "In fact, I'll call you when I get there because I want you to be on the phone when I launch a torpedo into your ridiculous assertion," he said.

"Suit yourself. We'll be waiting for your call," John said.

"I'll call you back in twenty minutes," Bob said.

John placed the telephone down on its cradle, and Captain Simpson said, "Since today's schedule is no longer applicable, what would you like me to do?"

"Let's wait for Bob to call back; we can bet that he will. And when he realizes we're not crazy, he'll be singing a different tune. In the meantime, here's what I'd ask you to do, Captain. After Bob calls back, I'd like you to take Sea Mist to Woods Hole empty—no passengers or vehicles. They'll most likely need an extra vessel to help alleviate the chaos that'll be created when the Islander arrives there," John said.

Chapter Thirteen

The Islander made the trip across Vineyard Sound in twenty-two minutes, less than half the time it usually takes. Clearly, the ferry had exceeded its top speed of 11.5 knots by leaps and bounds. What's more, passengers aboard the vessel enjoyed a customer service experience that harkened back to days of old—a time when customer satisfaction had meaning and was something for which to be proud.

The ferry was sparkling clean, both inside and out. Not a scrap of paper or trash could be found anywhere, and no graffiti was scribbled on walls or in the restrooms. Every crew member went above and beyond to treat all passengers on board with the utmost respect. The "old-school" method of doing business was a far cry from what today's customers are routinely subjected to: blatant incompetence; bad attitudes; a deep-rooted sense of superiority and entitlement. There was consensus among the passengers that a disproportionate number of C.F.C. employees were nothing but a collection of useless hacks and cronies that think they're doing you a favor by pilfering your hard-earned cash in exchange for poor service.

Bob Cunningham drove as fast as he could to the C.F.C. dock in Woods Hole. When he arrived, he haphazardly parked his car in the employee parking lot. He jumped out the car, and because he was in such a rush, ignored the fact that his car was occupying two parking spaces. At 6:17 a.m., he jogged to the end of the pier and looked toward the east. Minutes later, he heard a sound reminiscent of the now defunct Islander's air-horn. Though familiar, it sounded much more dissonant than he had remembered. And it shook him to his core.

In an attempt to rationalize what he had just heard, Bob surmised it to be another vessel with a similar-sounding horn. But when the stout ferry loomed as large as life and made a sharp turn to the starboard side as it coasted toward the dock, Bob could no longer deny it was the Islander. Its two steel doors were open, as wide as a whale's mouth, and she glided into the slip and gently bounced off the pilings before snuggling up against the ramp. Three crew members walked off the freight deck and secured the vessel, while several C.F.C. employees stood helplessly on the dock and witnessed something that, to them, was impossible.

Meanwhile, the freight vessel Ocean Spray, moored in an adjacent slip, was preparing to depart on the 7:00 a.m. trip to the Vineyard. However, after the Islander had arrived, all electrical power to the freight vessel was lost, similar to what had happened aboard Sea Mist in Vineyard Haven. Consequently, Ocean Spray was unable to make the trip.

Bob, in a state of shock, stood motionless on the dock. He reached into his pocket, grabbed hold of his cell phone, and dialed John's number.

"Hello, John? I don't know exactly how to say this, but you were right. A vessel that looks exactly like the Islander has docked…I'll have to call you back."

"Bob, it *is* the Islander," John said.

'Click,' went the phone.

"Hello? Hello?" Bob must've hung up," John said as he listened to the dial tone coming from the telephone handset.

After the Islander had arrived at Woods Hole, passengers walked briskly off the freight deck, just as countless others had done in the 1950s and 60s, prior to the use of gangways. Many of them appeared upbeat, even jovial, as they strolled off the vessel with a spring in their step. Elated by the quality of service they had received during the trip across Vineyard Sound, a barrage of accolades was levied upon this old, but new crew of the Islander. This was followed by countless smiles and nods of approval by every passenger that had disembarked from the vessel.

After the last vehicle drove off the ferry, a baggage cart—operated by an elderly crew member sporting a vintage C.F.C. uniform—circa 1950—slowly made its way over the ramp and came to a stop on the dock next to the slip. To look at them, it seemed as if every member of the crew was a senior citizen, between sixty and seventy-five years old.

At 6:45 a.m., the crew began to load vehicles and passengers onto the ferry. In a repeat performance of what had occurred on the Vineyard, the same gentleman that John had seen on the dock at Vineyard Haven greeted customers and collected tickets before directing the vehicles to his co-workers inside the vessel.

Just before the last car boarded, a raspy-sounding voice crackled over a loudspeaker attached to the outside wall of the ticket office.

Attention please. This is the last call for the seven o'clock ferry to Martha's Vineyard. I repeat...all aboard for the seven o'clock ferry to the Vineyard on the motor vessel Islander, departing from slip number 2.

Startled by what he had just heard, Bob snapped to attention and sprinted to the ticket office, only to find things in total disarray. No one seemed to know what was going on. Amidst flaring tempers, confusion, and long lines that extended out the door, the clerks at the ticket counter had had all they could handle, and then some.

"Who made that announcement?" Bob asked in a demanding tone.

The C.F.C. employees looked at each other, quizzical expressions on their faces.

"No one in here made the announcement," a counter clerk said.

"What are you talking about? That's ridiculous," Bob snapped. "Someone had to have made it!"

"Mr. Cunningham, what he says is true. The announcement didn't originate from this office. It seemed to have come through the loudspeakers on its own," a second clerk said.

"How's that possible? Somebody, anybody, please tell me what the hell is going on here?" Bob pleaded.

The clerks sat stoic while glancing at each other, desperately searching for an answer. It seemed that the only thing they could do was wear blank expressions on their faces and, out of frustration, shrug their shoulders.

Bob, now apoplectic, stormed out of the ticket office and sprinted back to the dock. But when he got there, the ferry Islander had already departed. He stood at the end of the pier and watched the vessel make a hard left turn to portside, and then chug toward towards Martha's Vineyard.

Chapter Fourteen

John sat quietly at his desk at the C.F.C. ferry terminal in Vineyard Haven, his emotions vacillating between inquisitiveness and disbelief. He desperately wanted to make some sense out of what was happening. It was almost as if he were immersed in an episode of *The Twilight Zone*. Just as he was about to pick up the telephone, it began to ring. He gazed at the telephone as if he were in a hypnotic trance, and then finally, after the tenth ring, answered the phone.

"John de Souza speaking, how may I help you?" he asked.

"John?"

"Yes?"

"John, Harold Grandly here. What's all this nonsense about the Islander?"

"Mr. Grandly, I was just about to call you," John said.

"Well, now that I've saved you the trouble, would you mind telling me what's going on?"

John paused and took a deep breath.

"I know this is going to sound crazy, Mr. Grandly, but the Islander has come back. Several C.F.C. employees, including myself, saw her."

"The Islander? Come back? John, if you'll recall, we sent Mr. Collins to New Jersey three days ago to witness the dismantling of the Islander. When he returned home, he brought back photographs he had taken of the vessel as it was ripped apart and hauled away. How could the ferry have just reappeared out of thin air?"

"I don't know the answer to that, Mr. Grandly. But what I *can* tell you is that *it is* the Islander...she's back. I saw her with my own eyes. And she's in pristine condition—brand spanking new—with not a dent or scratch anywhere," John said.

"Have you and Bob gone completely insane? What you're saying is impossible...it's pure nonsense."

"I can understand why you don't believe what I'm saying. I don't know whether to believe it myself. However, I can only tell you what I saw. And because of that, I'd suggest you see it for yourself. Not only has the Islander returned, she's assumed Island Gold's trips. In fact, she's due to arrive at Woods Hole at 10:45," John said.

"Bob and I will be there," Grandly said. "I'll call you when we get to the dock."

"Okay, Mr. Grandly. I'll wait to hear back from you. By the way, do you have any idea when the repairs on the Island Gold will be completed? When can we expect to get her back?" John asked.

Grandly paused, then said, "It's my understanding that the maintenance crew discovered additional mechanical problems with the vessel. It'll be at least another two weeks before she can return to service."

"Two weeks? How can I possibly cover that number of trips while she's in dry-docking?" John asked.

"That's your problem, John. Not mine. It's what you get paid the big bucks for," Grandly said.

Big Bucks? Yeah, right, John thought to himself.

"Thank God for the Islander," he mumbled to himself. *What am I saying? Can this really be happening?*

After John hung up the telephone, he heard the low timbre of the Islander's air horn announcing its arrival. John had no desire to grapple with the issue again, so, he closed his eyes and pressed both hands tightly against his ears in hopes that the sound would dissipate, and, along with it, the image of the old ferry gliding into the slip.

Though John had procrastinated for as long as he could, his curiosity was too strong to resist. He got up and walked over to the window. But, before he glanced outside, he stopped, took a deep breath, and then sheepishly peered through the dusty venetian blinds that looked as if they hadn't been cleaned in months. When he scanned the dock area, his worst fears were confirmed. The Islander had made the trip in twenty-two minutes, twice as fast as any vessel in the C.F.C. fleet.

After the ferry was secured to the dock, crew members disembarked and carried out their assigned tasks with diligence. Their movements seemed to be mechanical, machine-like, almost as if they were robots programmed to perform a variety of functions with utmost precision.

John was tempted to go aboard the vessel and investigate, but then decided against it because he knew that Mr. Grandly would not approve of his taking matters into his own hands. At least until such time that Mr. Grandly believed what John had told him, or that a decision had been made as to the best way to handle the situation. At that point, all John could do was go down to the dock and observe. Again, the only thing the perplexed C.F.C. dock workers could do was to stand there and watch the passengers and vehicles disembark.

Fifteen minutes later, another group of passengers boarded the ferry, unencumbered by C.F.C. employees.

At 10:00 a.m. sharp, the stout ferry pulled out of the slip, glided past the breakwater, and continued on to Woods Hole. Once again, passengers enjoyed a level of customer service that was sorely lacking at the boat line. The interior of the vessel was immaculate, and the crew members—in addition to being courteous and attentive in every respect—had also exceeded expectations by going above and beyond to deliver the best possible customer service to everyone on board.

John walked to the office and sat down at his desk. He thought about the shocking revelation that Mr. Grandly was about to get. He'd only wished he could be there to see the expression on the C.F.C. Board Chairman's face when the Islander sailed into the slip at Woods Hole.

Mr. Grandly and Bob Cunningham had decided to wait in the board room at the C.F.C. terminal until the ferry arrived. Even before he had seen it for himself, and, after having heard John's and Bob's accounts—not to mention the rumors swirling among C.F.C. employees—Mr. Grandly slowly began to accept the fact that neither John nor Bob, had gone insane, and that what they had told him was true.

"Bob, you *do* understand why I'm hesitant to believe any of this, don't you?" Mr. Grandly asked.

"Yes, I understand," Bob said. "If I hadn't seen it for myself, I'd be apprehensive, too."

"It's almost half past ten—we'd better get to the dock. I hope this isn't some silly prank," Mr. Grandly said, in a skeptical tone.

Moments later, they left the office. When they arrived at the dock, a huge crowd had already gathered there. Apparently, the rumor mill had churned out a plethora of stories that had spread like wildfire. Hordes of spectators were milling about, eager to catch a glimpse of the so-called ghost ship, which, if true, was poised to wreak havoc on C.F.C. operations.

After they had wended their ways through throngs of people, Mr. Grandly and Bob Cunningham stood at the end of the pier and looked toward the southeast. In the distance—Martha's Vineyard and the Elizabeth Islands in the background—a vessel made its approach. The angle of the sun had caused a blinding beam of light to reflect off something on the ferry, obscuring the view of those watching it chug towards Woods Hole.

Within seconds of having seen a vessel that looked eerily similar to the Islander, Mr. Grandly dashed through the crowd and headed for the ramp to watch it arrive. Bob followed behind as best he could, but became lost in a sea of wide-eyed spectators who were astonished by what they saw.

The Islander coasted effortlessly across the water and toward the dock, but, before snuggling into the slip, the captain directed the crew in the engine room to shift the diesel engines into reverse. The engines roared, causing a billow of light-blue smoke to rise from a beige smokestack on the upper deck of the vessel. The pungent odor of diesel fuel wafted in the air, and wisps of white foam—floating atop the churning, bluish-green saltwater—spewed against the pilings before slowing down the ferry. Finally, the stout vessel gently nudged the ramp and came to a stop.

Once again, the same three crew members sauntered off the ferry—just as they had done earlier that day—and smiled as they went about their busywork. However, Mr. Grandly wasn't content to just stand there and do nothing.

"Hey, you! Yes, I'm talking to you," Mr. Grandly said to a crew member who happened to be hand-cranking a mechanism that tightened a steel cable to the hull of the ferry. The man stopped what he was doing, looked at Mr. Grandly, and said, "How can I help you, sir?"

"You can begin by telling me what's going on here," Grandly said.

"I'm sorry, sir. I don't mean to be coy, but I don't understand your question," the man said.

"Who are you?" Mr. Grandly asked in a condescending tone.

The man smiled and politely answered, "My name's Manny Barboza. I'm a crew member aboard the motor vessel Islander...been so since 1950."

"Since 1950, huh? Well, Mr. Barboza, in case you haven't noticed, its 2011, and what you're doing here is illegal. This vessel is no longer in the C.F.C. fleet, and none of its crew members are authorized to work as employees of the C.F.C.

Manny, unfazed by what Mr. Grandly had said, maintained a pleasant demeanor, though he looked at Mr. Grandly with a curious expression on his face.

"I'd like to speak with the captain. What's his name?" Mr. Grandly asked.

"Black. His name's Captain Sigmund Black," Manny answered.

Mr. Grandly, flummoxed and red-faced, looked directly at Mr. Barboza, and says, "Listen, buddy. Tell the captain, Mr. Black, that the chairman of the C.F.C. Board would like to have a word with him—NOW!"

"I'm sorry sir, but I'm not at liberty to do that."

"Is that so? And may I ask why not?" Grandly replied,

now having gotten to within inches of Manny Barboza's face.

"Pardon me, sir. There's really no need to get aflutter. Captain Black is master of this vessel, and we've been instructed not to disturb him."

"I don't give a damn about your instructions. I demand to see the captain!" Mr. Grandly barked.

"I'm afraid that's impossible, sir."

"What are you talking about? If you don't comply with my request, then I'll have a good reason to have you *and* the rest of your crew arrested," Mr. Grandly said in a threatening tone.

Manny maintained his composure. He didn't flinch or overreact. Instead, he nonchalantly looked Mr. Grandly straight in the eye, and, in a calm voice, said, "Sir, I'd like to continue our conversation, but we're on a tight schedule, and, as you know, we can't be late. So, if you'll excuse me, I've got to get back to work."

Mr. Barboza turned and walked down the ramp and onto the ferry, only to be followed by two other crew members. Minutes later, they directed vehicles and passengers off the ferry and prepared to board those waiting on the dock for the trip back to the Vineyard. Mr. Grandly, seemingly taken aback by what had just occurred, stood there momentarily before walking toward the open doors on the freight deck. But suddenly, Bob grabbed his arm and held him back before he could go aboard.

"Please, Mr. Grandly. This isn't the best way to deal with the situation. We should get law enforcement involved because there's no telling what might happen if we attempt to intervene without assistance," Bob said.

"Perhaps you're right, Bob. I'll go inside and call a friend of mine at the State Police. Also, I'm going to convene an emergency meeting this evening with the rest of the C.F.C. board members. Hopefully, we'll be able to decide how to resolve this problem. Please inform John de Souza about the meeting," Mr. Grandly said.

"Will do," Bob said.

Mr. Grandly made his way to the boardroom on the second floor of the C.F.C. ticket office and sat at the head of a polished mahogany table. As he looked down at the table, he couldn't help but notice his reflection staring back at him. What struck him were three jagged lines that ran across his forehead. They reminded him of electrical wires suspended between two telephone poles, intimating the telltale sign of the stress he felt building up inside. Getting back to the task at hand, Mr. Grandly reached for the telephone and dialed the Massachusetts State Police, in Bourne.

"Hello, State Police—Bourne barracks. Trooper Johnson speaking, how can I help you?"

"Trooper Johnson, this is Harold Grandly from the Commonwealth Ferryboat Company in Woods Hole. I'd like to speak with Major Steven Smith. It's very important. Is he available?"

"Please hold, Mr. Grandly. I'll transfer you to the Major," the trooper said.

"Thanks."

Though it took only minutes for Major Smith to answer the phone; Mr. Grandly felt as if an hour had passed.

"Hello, Harold. What can I do for you?" Major Smith asked.

"Steve, I've got an emergency situation on my hands, and I need your help."

"What is it?"

"I don't know quite how to say this, but I think we've got a ghost ship on our hands," Mr. Grandly said.

"Did you say ghost ship? What do you mean?"

"It's the ferry Islander. She's sailing the Woods Hole-Martha's Vineyard route again. I saw her myself," he said.

Major Smith paused, and then said, "I thought she'd been scrapped earlier this week."

"That was my understanding also. But it seems that that's not the case. I'd have to guess she wasn't scrapped; she couldn't have been."

"Are you sure?"

"Absolutely," Mr. Grandly replied.

Major Smith paused again, seemingly at a loss for words.

"Did you attempt to board the vessel?" he asked.

"No. I thought it best to call you first," he said.

"How can I help, Harold?"

"If at all possible, I'd appreciate it if you could send a few of your troopers to Woods Hole as soon as you can. I'm convening an emergency meeting with the C.F.C. board members tonight at 7:30. We hope to come up with a plan about how to deal with this anomaly. As to your question about boarding the vessel...I'd like to go aboard her but wouldn't want to attempt that without the assistance of law enforcement."

"I understand, Harold. I'll assign six troopers to the C.F.C. dock right away."

"Thanks, Steve. I'd really appreciate that."

"Sure, no problem," Major Smith said.

Mr. Grandly lay the telephone down on its cradle, but then picked it up again and called each board member to tell them about the meeting that evening. Bob Cunningham had advised John de Souza, and John confirmed his attendance.

It might have been by sheer coincidence, but everyone who had planned to attend the meeting had arrived early. Even John, who had taken an earlier ferry from the Vineyard than he otherwise would have, walked into the boardroom at 6:00 p.m., a full hour and a half before the meeting was scheduled to begin.

To look at them, it seemed as if every board member felt apprehensive. They exhibited emotions that ran the full gamut: curiosity; wonderment; disbelief; fear of the unknown; denial.

Mr. Grandly could almost feel the discontent in the room; it weighed on him like a ton of bricks. But as board chairman, it was his responsibility to manage the situation and allay any feelings of consternation.

Prior to the meeting, Chairman Grandly had had light refreshments delivered. The fare included mini-sandwiches: tuna; chicken salad; turkey. Also, he had ordered cheese and crackers, chips and dip, assorted Danish, cookies, soft drinks, coffee, and tea.

At prior meetings, the food would have been gobbled up in short order by opportunistic board members scrounging for a free meal. But, tonight, the food sat on the table, untouched. It seemed as if there was no interest in the refreshments, except for several houseflies that sporadically buzzed about, dive-bombing the sandwiches and pastries in relentless fashion, attempting to alight on them.

At approximately 7:05 p.m., Mr. Grandly gaveled the meeting to order.

"Good evening, everyone. I appreciate you being here on such short notice. I know it's still early, but since everyone's here, I'd like to get started."

He paused, looked around the room, a stern expression on his face, and said, "There's a matter of critical importance that I must bring to your attention. And it involves all of us."

At first, a soft murmur wafted about the room. And then an increasingly audible chatter bubbled up from among the board members.

After having shared the news with the board of directors about the Islander and the fact that it was once again sailing the high seas, their response was incredulous.

"Come on, Harold. How's that possible?" a board member interjected amongst the babble.

"I don't know how it happened, and I certainly can't tell you why. But, there's one thing I do know…it *has* happened… the Islander is back. I saw her myself," Mr. Grandly said.

"This is preposterous!" a second board member blurted out in disbelief as he banged his fist on the table.

"I think we all agree with you, Mr. Callahan. But whether you choose to believe it or not, it's a fact. The Islander has returned, and has done so in all her glory," Mr. Grandly said.

"But Mr. Chairman, just yesterday, I flipped through an album full of photos showing the ferry being ripped apart by a huge crane, bolt by bolt. Sheets of the Islander's outer skin were peeled away as if it were an onion, right down to its steel hull and beam, which now lay abandoned in a ship graveyard at Port Newark, New Jersey," said a third board member.

The murmuring continued, albeit much louder. It reverberated throughout the room. Everyone looked at each other in search of an explanation—any explanation. Because what they had heard had defied logic.

"Mr. de Souza was the first to see the Islander this morning. John, would you be so kind as to share with the board what you saw?" Mr. Grandly asked.

"Of course, Mr. Grandly," he said.

John stood. But before he spoke, he glanced around the room, and in a wavering voice, said, "This morning, at approximately five o'clock, I arrived at the office in Vineyard Haven, just as I've done every workday in the past. The fog in the harbor was thick; it almost looked like a huge woolen blanket had been spread over the island. In fact, I could hardly see the wharf. But when I looked closer, I saw what I thought was the Islander berthed in slip number one. But I knew it couldn't have been the ferry because, as we all know, she was dismantled earlier this week."

"Sounds to me like you'd had one too many cocktails," mocked Sam Solomon, one of the board members.

Mr. Grandly stared at Sam, and said, "That'll be enough out of you, Mr. Solomon. This isn't a joke. It's a very serious matter, and we must find a way to deal with it. Please continue, John."

John briefly hesitated as he attempted to collect his thoughts, similar to a child that had been reprimanded by a parent, only to be asked to explain why they had misbehaved.

John continued.

"Though stunned by the presence of the ferry, I had decided to approach it, nevertheless. I walked down the ramp that led to the freight deck and peered inside. The vessel was empty. However, I could hear the distinctive low rumble from its diesel engines," John said.

"Did you attempt to go aboard?" another board member asked.

"No, I didn't. I was taken aback, confused. I didn't believe what I saw. At first, I thought I was hallucinating. But then I decided to go back to my office. Shortly thereafter, I heard the usual sounds I was accustomed to hearing at the dock. I looked out the window and noticed three elderly men loading vehicles and passengers onto the ferry. That's when I realized I wasn't hallucinating.

John paused and grabbed hold of a pitcher on the table. He filled a paper cup with water, then set the pitcher back down and took a sip from the cup.

"Please continue, John," Mr. Grandly said.

"The crew of the freight vessel Sea Mist had arrived at work, and we stood on the dock and watched passengers and vehicles board the Islander. I had even had a conversation with one of the crew members while this was occurring. The gentleman standing on the ramp possessed a demeanor that was courteous, very respectful. He told me, in no uncertain terms, that they were preparing to make the 6:00 a.m. trip to Woods Hole.

"What did you say to him after he had said that?" Mr. Grandly asked.

"To be honest, I didn't know what to say; I felt flabbergasted."

"Well, did you ask who he was or where he'd come from?" Bob Cunningham asked.

"Yes, but he didn't respond. He simply went about the business of collecting tickets and loading vehicles onto the ferry."

"Now, John, do you *really* expect us to believe that cockamamie story? Could any of it be true?" Mr. Solomon asked.

John looked squarely at the man. "Mr. Solomon, whether you choose to believe what I'm saying, or not, is immaterial. I'm simply telling you my account of what happened, that's all," he said in a stern voice that clearly elucidated his frustration.

Mr. Grandly, annoyed by Mr. Solomon's rude accusations, stared at him with his black, beady eyes and a scowl on his face. It was obvious that he didn't appreciate the manner in which Mr. Solomon had badgered John and continued to question the sincerity of his story.

"Please go on, John," Mr. Grandly said.

"After having failed to elicit a response from the gentleman, I walked back to my office, only to be told that the ferry, Sea Mist, had lost power. Somehow, the presence of the Islander had caused a power outage aboard the Sea Mist. She appeared to be dead in the water. And that's when I placed a call to Bob Cunningham," John said.

"Is that what happened, Bob?" Mr. Grandly asked.

"Yes," Bob replied, nodding his head in the affirmative. "After the Islander had left the Vineyard, John called to tell me when she'd arrive at Woods Hole. At first, I didn't believe him. I thought he'd lost his mind. That was, until I saw the ferry for myself. And it was just as John had described. The vessel arrived with a full load of vehicles and passengers. After it had been unloaded, the crew loaded up again for the return trip to the Vineyard. As impossible as it might seem, the Islander is operating on her own volition. And she's immune to any attempt to intervene."

John continued.

"What's more, she's been transporting passengers and vehicles between Woods Hole and the Vineyard since early this morning."

"It sounds like something out of a Stephen King novel," Bob said.

"Yes. But in this case, it's real," John replied.

After John and Bob had shared their stories with members of the board, Mr. Grandly said, "Bob called me and conveyed the same story. Similar to how he had reacted to John, I thought he was joking. But then, Bob and I went to the dock and watched the Islander glide into the slip. And let me be clear...it *was* the Islander. When I attempted to confront the crew members, I was shunned. They didn't honor my request to speak with the captain. It was at that point that I called the State Police to request assistance because Bob, John, and I plan to go aboard the ferry tomorrow morning. The Bourne State Police are sending over six troopers. I just need to let them know what time to be here."

A lengthy discussion ensued about the pros and cons of attempting to stop the Islander's rogue activities. However, in the end, the C.F.C. Board unanimously decided the best course of action to take was to commandeer the vessel. Also, they felt that sitting on the sidelines and doing nothing was no longer an option. What's more, the board members knew it would be impetuous to allow this activity to continue, not to mention that if they failed to act, they'd be accused of wanton dereliction of duty.

When the meeting ended, everyone bolted from the boardroom. Mr. Grandly stayed behind to mull over the decision that had been reached. He wasn't so much concerned about the decision, for he understood something had to be done. Rather, it was more of whether the board's aggressive stance would achieve the desired result.

Before leaving the boardroom, Mr. Grandly called Major Smith at the State Police barracks to request that his troopers report to the dock at 5:30 the following morning. That way, they'd be ready to handle any problems that might occur when the Islander arrives from the Vineyard. Major Smith told Mr. Grandly that he had alerted the Coast Guard and that they would be available to assist, if needed.

More than likely few, if any, of the board members slept soundly that night. And it was a good bet that Mr. Grandly, Bob Cunningham, and John de Souza experienced simultaneous bouts of insomnia that kept them awake for the entire night.

At 5:12 the next morning, Mr. Grandly, Bob, John, and Captain Simpson met at the C.F.C. dock in Woods Hole. They were surprised by the number of vehicles waiting in line to board the first ferry to the Vineyard.

Bob took inventory of the cars and trucks, and said, "There must be at least seventy-five vehicles waiting to board. Highly unusual for this time of day."

John and Captain Simpson nodded in agreement. However, Mr. Grandly seemed disinterested, or deep in thought, distracted by something to which only he was privy. Or perhaps he simply didn't hear Bob. More than likely, he chose to ignore him.

As soon as they entered the ticket office, Mr. Grandly said, "I'll be back; I'm going to use the restroom. I'll meet you gentlemen in the conference room in a few minutes."

"Okay. We'll see you there," Bob replied.

Clutching his abdomen with both hands, Mr. Grandly made a beeline to the men's restroom. His stomach felt as if it were tied up in knots. He rushed into a stall, pulled down his slacks and boxer shorts and sat down on the cold toilet seat that felt as if it had been carved out of a block of ice, causing his buttocks to cling to the seat like Velcro. To ease the stabbing pain in his gut, he leaned forward as far as he could and applied pressure to his abdomen.

No relief.

As he sat there, thoughts of the dilemma that the C.F.C. faced had made his nausea seem miniscule in comparison. Also, he realized that, as chairman of the board, it was his responsibility to find a solution to the problem.

Could this be retribution for having circumvented the bidding process and awarding the new ferry contract to the Mississippi Dry-Dock Company? He wondered. *And what, if anything, do John de Souza and Bob Cunningham know? Did Senate President William Clay share with anyone what I had done? And, if so, will I be prosecuted and sent to prison?*

A flood of questions ricocheted in his head like a bullet that had been fired into a room made of steel walls. The burden was too heavy for him to bear. And though he tried to force the thoughts from his mind, he found it all but impossible.

By now, Mr. Grandly was beyond overwhelmed. Beads of sweat had begun to form on his forehead, making the nauseated feeling in his stomach seem even more acute. He attempted to stand, only to drop to his knees in front of the toilet bowl, as if praying to a porcelain God.

Moments later, his stomach heaved, and he leaned over the toilet bowl and retched. The rancid odor wafted up his nostrils and only compounded the churning he felt in his stomach, like clothes tumbling in a dryer. He glanced down at his crisp white shirt, only to see that it had been soiled by vomit. After he had finished his business and been weakened by the whole ordeal, he flushed the toilet and slowly trudged over to the sink to wash his face and hands. But before doing so, he grabbed hold of a miniature bottle of mouthwash that sat on the counter and gargled with the minty-green liquid to rid himself of bad breath and the foul taste in his mouth.

Just as Mr. Grandly was about to leave the restroom, he happened to catch a glimpse of his reflection in a mirror hanging on the wall above the sink. Surprised by how sallow his face appeared, he let out a sigh and adjusted his comb-over to hide the gaping bald spot atop his head. He glanced in the mirror one last time, then opened the door and walked out.

More than twenty minutes had elapsed since Mr. Grandly had gone to the restroom. He stumbled into the conference room, only to find Bob, John, and Captain Simpson seated around the table, quizzical expressions on their faces.

"We were wondering what had happened to you, Harold. Where've you been?" Bob asked.

"I spent more time in the men's room than I had planned. My stomach feels kind of queasy," Mr. Grandly said.

"Your face looks pale, white as a ghost. Are you feeling all right?" John asked.

"I'm fine, thanks. I think I just need some fresh air," he answered.

Bob walked over to the window to open it, but then looked outside. "The State Police have arrived—six troopers, in three vehicles. Boy, they're not fooling around," he said.

"Major Smith assured me that he was going to send them over to assist, in case we need them," Mr. Grandly said.

I hope not, John thought to himself.

"We'd best get downstairs," Bob said.

Mr. Grandly scurried ahead of the others. He seemed eager to share his plan with the troopers.

Prior to the Islander's arrival at Woods Hole, the troopers positioned themselves on the ramp, three on each side, while Mr. Grandly, Bob, and John waited on the dock.

As the Islander approached the dock, its powerful engines slowed down the ferry to a point where its hull gently kissed the ramp. And, like clockwork, three crew members disembarked and secured the vessel to the dock.

When the elderly ticket taker, Manny Barboza, shuffled off the ferry, Mr. Grandly hurried over to meet him. He nodded to the troopers, and then confronted Mr. Barboza.

"Excuse me, sir. I don't know if you remember me, but I'm Harold Grandly, Chairman of the Board of Directors at the Commonwealth Ferryboat Company."

The old man peered at Mr. Grandly with a wary eye, and said, "Yes, I know who you are."

"Well then, you must know why I'm here."

"No, sir, I can't say that I do," Mr. Barboza replied.

"Please allow me to refresh your memory, Mr. Barboza… it *is* Mr. Barboza, isn't it?"

"Yes, that's correct," he said.

"My associates and I would like to come aboard the ferry. And we intend to do just that…with, or without your permission." He continued. "Now, as you can see, Mr. Barboza, we've got the full support of the Massachusetts State Police, and they're here to ensure that you comply with my request to board this vessel," Mr. Grandly said.

At that moment, the state troopers assumed an aggressive stance that resembled a human blockade, ready to spring into action.

"Mr. Grandly, sir, we don't want to cause any trouble. All we want is to do our job, nothing more," Mr. Barboza said.

"Good," Mr. Grandly said. "Then there should be no problem."

"Hey, Manny! Come on, man...we've got to unload these vehicles," a crew member yelled from inside the ferry.

"All right...All right," Mr. Barboza answered.

He turned toward Mr. Grandly, and politely said, "Excuse me, sir, but I must get back to work."

No sooner than Mr. Barboza had finished speaking, cars and trucks had begun to roll off the ferry. Mr. Grandly and the state troopers, after having been forced off the ramp, dashed over to where John, Bob, and Captain Simpson were standing. Soon, the freight deck was empty, and a crew member began to direct more vehicles toward the ferry.

"Now hold on a minute!" Mr. Grandly shouted as he made his way back to the ramp, the troopers following closely behind. But it was too late. The loading of the ferry had already commenced.

Mr. Barboza watched as the troopers approached the ramp in lockstep. He warned them to stand clear, lest they get injured by the moving vehicles.

Three troopers stood side-by-side and blocked the path of an oncoming car. One of the troopers pointed at Mr. Barboza, and said, "Excuse me, sir. If you don't stop what you're doing, RIGHT NOW, I'll arrest you for refusing to obey a Massachusetts State Police Trooper."

Mr. Barboza, unfazed by the trooper's directive, calmly stood there and grinned. He then turned and waved the car aboard the ferry, ignoring the trooper. In order to avoid being run over, the trooper climbed over the railing and balanced himself on the outside of the ramp while holding on to a steel cable.

At that point, Mr. Grandly had become apoplectic. Now more determined than ever to board the ferry, he walked briskly down the ramp. But, when he reached the door to the freight deck, he suddenly stopped. Though he attempted to, he was unable to board the vessel. It was as if an invisible tether kept him from going aboard. He bounced backwards, similar to how someone inadvertently walks into a glass door, not knowing that the door is closed.

Meanwhile, passengers and vehicles continued to make their way onto the Islander, until finally; she was filled with over five-hundred passengers, fifty-seven cars, two tractor-trailers, and a tour bus. Although the scene at the dock was hectic, the crew methodically went about the task of loading the ferry. Mr. Grandly and the State Police had done all they could to prevent the Islander from leaving the dock.

Just as two crew members walked off the ferry to release it from the ramp, three State Police troopers sprang into action. "You're under arrest—all three of you," one of the troopers said as they approached the men with guns drawn and handcuffs at the ready. But when they attempted to handcuff the three men, they found that they could not. Neither handcuffs nor the threat of using lethal force had had any effect. And when the troopers attempted to grab hold of the crew members, their hands seemed to pass through what appeared to be astral projections, or, bodies devoid of physical mass. Not only did the crew possess the ability to defy the laws of physics, they also seemed able to manipulate time and space as well.

Throughout the scuffle, the crew members kept their composure. They smiled, as if in a state of eternal bliss, and released the ferry from the ramp while Manny Barboza—after having collected passenger tickets and vehicle boarding passes—lazily strolled back onto the freight deck.

Minutes later, the stout ferry made its way out of the slip, leaving Mr. Grandly and the State Police troopers standing impotently on the dock. They looked at one another, dumbfounded, and in a state of shock. A trooper then said, "I'll contact the Coast Guard. Perhaps they'll be able to intercept the vessel at sea."

Don't waste your time, John de Souza thought as he smirked with satisfaction.

While attempting to understand how the resurrection of the Islander had come to pass, John felt a renewed sense of hope. Perhaps there's some intrinsic value in all of this. *Somehow, I know there's a reason why the Islander has come back,* he thought. John found himself rooting for the old ferry like an anonymous supporter, secretly cheerleading from the sidelines.

Chapter Fifteen

Not long after the State Police had contacted the Coast Guard, they dispatched a cutter to intercept the Islander and it caught up with the ferry midway between Woods Hole and the Vineyard. As the cutter sailed alongside the Islander, an announcement was made over a loudspeaker. "Attention…attention, motor vessel Islander. This is the United States Coast Guard. You are hereby ordered to stop and drop anchor…I repeat…stop and drop your anchor and prepare to be boarded."

Captain Black dismissed the order and continued to pilot the ferry toward the Vineyard. In fact, he increased the speed of the vessel to where the cutter could barely keep up. And by the time the Islander had rounded West Chop and entered Vineyard Haven Harbor, the Coast Guard cutter had fallen two miles behind. The crew aboard the cutter, having realized that any attempt to stop the ferry was futile, requested permission to stand down. Shortly thereafter, the cutter ended its pursuit and returned to Falmouth.

The C.F.C. Board of Directors decided that it was not prudent to attempt further action against the Islander and her crew while docked at Vineyard Haven. They thought it better to wait until the vessel returned to Woods Hole. And, as was the case since the ferry had miraculously risen from the scrapheap, the stout ferryboat, once again loaded with vehicles and passengers, departed the island.

When the Islander arrived at Woods Hole, Mr. Grandly, Bob Cunningham, John de Souza, Captain Simpson, and the State Police were waiting at the dock. This time, however, Mr. Grandly decided to take a diplomatic approach.

He walked on to the ramp and initiated a friendly conversation with the ticket taker. "Mr. Barboza, I'd like to apologize for the misunderstanding that occurred when we last spoke," he said.

"Misunderstanding? What misunderstanding?" Mr. Barboza asked, with a wide smile.

How can this guy be so pleasant? Mr. Grandly wondered.

"It's just that my associates and I would like to come aboard and observe how you provide such great customer service. Perhaps we could learn a few things," Mr. Grandly continued, in an upbeat, albeit insincere tone.

"That'll be fine. But if you plan to travel to the Vineyard aboard the Islander, then each of you will have to purchase a passenger ticket. There are no free passes, not even for C.F.C. employees," Mr. Barboza said.

Grandly was taken aback by what Mr. Barboza had said.

"Excuse me? But management always rides for free," he replied.

"Not if you want to travel aboard *this* ferry, sir! You see, Mr. Grandly, there's no favoritism, nepotism, or special treatment for those who ride on the Islander. The only exceptions are for Veterans, disabled individuals, senior citizens, and children under five years old. So, if you and your associates plan to travel with us, then I'd suggest you purchase your tickets right away because we'll be departing soon," Mr. Barboza said as he continued to collect tickets and wave cars aboard.

"What? You mean to tell me that you let all those people ride for *free?* We only allow children under five to ride for free. Veterans, the disabled, and senior citizens get a 10% discount, but they don't get a free ride," Mr. Grandly said.

Now more determined than ever, Mr. Grandly continues to plead his case, but Mr. Barboza was having none of it; he was adamant about Mr. Grandly and his comrades not boarding without first purchasing a ticket.

After several minutes of bickering back and forth, Mr. Grandly finally conceded, and, reluctantly, he led the others to the ticket office to purchase their passenger tickets. They then scurried back to the ramp, handed over their tickets, and walked on to the ferry. However, once aboard the vessel, they were astonished by what they saw.

It was obvious that courtesy, cleanliness, and exemplary customer service was something the entire crew of the Islander emulated. The concept was by no means rocket science. Also, the crew believed that exceptional customer service was the bedrock of success and something for which to be proud.

Mr. Grandly and his associates climbed the stairs from the freight deck to the upper level and stopped at the lunch counter. Besides being as clean as a hospital operating room, the refreshing odor of pine-scented cleaning solvents wafted throughout. The food and beverages for sale were of the highest quality, not the bottom-of-the-barrel culinary offerings peddled on the other ferries. And the price for the food was more than reasonable. In fact, it was a steal by today's standards.

"I'm hungry," Bob said, as he salivated while looking at the plump, juicy hot dogs rotating on a rotisserie. "I'll take a chili-dog, loaded," he said to an older female standing behind the counter.

"How can you think of food at a time like this?" Mr. Grandly asked.

"Hey, a man's gotta eat, you know?" Bob said.

Grandly looked at him and frowned.

"I must admit, everything looks so much more appealing than what I'm used to seeing on the other vessels," John said.

The woman handed Bob a foot-long hot dog, the warm, soft bun overflowing with black beans, salsa, jalapeno peppers, onions, and topped with sour cream. "That'll be fifteen cents, sir," she said.

"Fifteen cents? Are you sure?" Bob inquired, in disbelief.

"Yes, sir."

"Wow! This is what a hot dog would've cost fifty years ago," Bob said.

"Holy mackerel! We charge $4.50 for a hot dog nowadays, and they're made with cheap fillers and are loaded with preservatives, and a host of inferior ingredients. What's more, that doesn't even include the condiments, for which we charge extra. But Bob, your dog looks to be 100% beef!" Captain Simpson said.

"And that's not all. Look at these prices! A soda fountain drink costs only a nickel, and you can get a fresh, quarter-pound hamburger grilled to perfection for twenty cents, not the thin, flat-as-a-pancake, frozen patties we sell for $5.50. And check this out…candy bars cost only three cents, and they're full-sized bars—not the miniature candy bars that we sell today," John said.

"Gentleman, I can appreciate your exuberance regarding the quality of the food and how inexpensive it is, but, let me remind you that we're here for a very important reason. We've got to get to the wheelhouse...now! Let's go," Grandly said.

Bob wolfed down his hot dog and, while eating as fast as he could, he inadvertently spilled chili sauce on his white shirt.

"How was your dog?" John asked as they made their way out of the lunch counter.

"Simply delicious," he answered.

"It must have been because you're wearing some of it," John said, jokingly.

Mr. Grandly led the way to the wheelhouse in a manner that mimicked a scene out of *Mutiny on the Bounty.* He had high hopes of overpowering Captain Black and his first mate and taking control of the vessel. Mr. Grandly's only reason for bringing Captain Simpson along was because of his years of experience piloting ferries, which would be needed to navigate the vessel to the Coast Guard station in Falmouth.

When they reached the wheelhouse, the door was ajar, so they climbed the five steel steps and walked inside. Mr. Grandly's objective was to commandeer the ferry.

"Good day, gentlemen. Please come in. We've been expecting you," said Captain Black. The men entered the wheelhouse and sat on four tall stools.

"You've been expecting us?" Mr. Grandly responded, with surprise.

"Why, yes, of course. How else do you think you got aboard?" the captain asked.

Captain Black, a man who possessed a diminutive physique, olive-colored skin, full head of silver-white hair and a black and gray mustache, greeted the men with a warm smile.

In order to get a clear view while piloting the ferry, he sat in the captain's chair, propped-up by three thick seat cushions. The epaulet stripes sewn on either shoulder of his uniform seemed to emit an amber glow, almost as if illuminated by a neon light that was visible even during the day.

Mr. Grandly, Bob, John, and Mr. Simpson, seemingly mesmerized by the stripes on Captain Black's uniform, suddenly snapped out of what appeared to be a hypnotic trance. First Mate Lance Monticello took control of the helm and guided the ferry toward Vineyard Haven Harbor while the captain conversed with his uninvited guests.

"Now, how can we be of service to you and your comrades, Mr. Grandly?"

"You know who I am?" Mr. Grandly asked.

"Yes, I do. Mr. Barboza told me all about you."

"Do you mean the older gentleman on the freight deck who collected our tickets?"

"Yes, Mr. Grandly. Mr. Barboza is our Purser," the captain said.

Mr. Grandly, Bob, John, and Captain Simpson sat there in awe. They still couldn't believe that they were aboard the Islander and headed for the Vineyard.

"Now, what can we do for you?" Captain Black asked again.

"You can begin by explaining what you're doing here. We know it's not possible for us to be on the Islander. She was disassembled and scrapped four days ago. And what I find even more astounding, Captain Black, is that you and your crew worked on this vessel over fifty years ago. What's more, all of you, except for one Joseph Silva—who has since retired—are deceased. So, logically, it's impossible for you to be here now," Mr. Grandly said.

The captain looked at his first mate and smiled.

Mr. Grandly continued.

"I went so far as to check the C.F.C. Human Resource's records. It states that you were the skipper aboard the Islander from 1950 to 1975."

"That would be correct, sir," the captain said, a Cheshire cat-like grin on his face. "It's good to know that the C.F.C has at least kept accurate records of past employees."

"I also happen to know that you passed away in June, 1985 of complications from emphysema. So, how could you possibly be here now?"

The captain glanced at his first mate, smiled again, and said, "Those damn cigarettes will do you in every time! Ain't that right, Monty?"

They both let out a hearty laugh. The captain then turned toward Mr. Grandly, looked him straight in the eye, and said, in a serious tone, "Are you and your associates not aboard this ship?"

"Yes, it appears that we are," Mr. Grandly said.

"Is this ship not carrying vehicles and passengers? And, are we not on our way to the Vineyard, Mr. Grandly?"

Grandly peers out the window and sees that the vessel is moving forward, slightly rocking from side to side as it glides over the ocean's surface. Also, he notices a flag attached to a pole on the bow fluttering in the wind. He then looks up, only to see several seagulls flying above, keeping pace with the ferry, in hopes that a passenger might toss a morsel of food their way.

"Yes," he said in a muted tone, a forlorn expression on his face.

"Well then, I guess we can all agree that we're here, and that we're on our way to the Vineyard," the captain said.

"Apparently, there's no refuting that fact," Mr. Grandly said, flush with embarrassment as he looked at Bob, John, and Captain Simpson before he lowered his head and stared at the floor.

"Let me explain to you why we're here," Captain Black said. "You see, Mr. Grandly, there's something drastically amiss at the Commonwealth Ferryboat Company today. It's nothing like it used to be back in the 1950s and 60s, when my crew and I proudly served aboard this vessel. We were honored to have worked on this beloved ferry, and believe it or not, she had reciprocated in kind by working tirelessly month after month, and year after year for decades, through all types of weather. It didn't matter whether she faced rain, sleet, hail, snow, or gale-force winds…the Islander was always ready, willing, and able.

However, not long after our time here had passed, something untoward had happened. The C.F.C. became a victim of its own success. Today, management seems more interested in turning a profit than providing customers with the best possible service. And, in the process, the company seems to have lost its way. I find it quite disheartening that the C.F.C. is not only motivated by the almighty dollar; but it's also being consumed by greed, disintegrating from within. To be frank, Mr. Grandly, it's all about the money. But what I find most offensive is that the C.F.C. displays no conscience when it comes to picking its customer's pockets in exchange for shoddy service. It's a damn shame," he said.

Mr. Grandly interjected, "I beg your pardon, captain. The C.F.C. provides a valuable service to its customers and does so at a reasonable cost."

"I'm sorry, but I must respectfully disagree. There's too much of an 'I've got to take care of my own' mentality at this boat line. Let's consider a few facts, shall we? First, the reality is that many people employed at the C.F.C. are composed of family members and friends or, as I like to call them... hacks...whose primary objective is to curry favor and earn a paycheck. But then again, they're not actually *earning* their salary; they're simply getting paid. Second, they couldn't care less about the customer. And third, the fact that most of them haven't a clue as to how to competently perform their jobs is a disgrace," the captain said.

Embarrassed, the four men displayed looks of bewilderment on their faces. They knew there was no way to refute the inherent truth in the captain's scathing assessment.

Despite knowing about a tried and true business philosophy that has withstood the test of time, Grandly, Cunningham, and Captain Simpson would hear none of it. John, the lone dissenter, recognized the nuggets of wisdom in what Captain Black had said.

"You know, Captain Black is absolutely correct," John said. "There *are* merits to treating your customers well. I've seen it in action, and it works."

If looks could kill, then John would have dropped dead on the floor right then and there. Mr. Grandly stared at him as if he'd morphed into an extraterrestrial being from another planet. He then displayed a mean scowl as if he were trying to convey to John, by way of telepathy or body language, to be quiet. Apparently, John had received the subliminal message because he suddenly stopped talking and bowed his head like an admonished child. He didn't utter another word.

Mr. Grandly stood, and said, "That's all well and good captain, but I'm here to inform you that we're taking control of this ferry. You have no authority to operate this vessel. Now,

I don't know how you're managing to pull this off, whether through black magic, voodoo, or by some other phenomena, but, as far as the C.F.C. is concerned, we're authorized to put an end to this phantom ship's rogue activities."

Despite Mr. Grandly's attempt at being forceful, the captain turns to him, and says, "I hate to disappoint you and your associates, but you have no control over this ferry, or her crew. What we're doing here is out of your purview."

"Really? We'll see about that."

Mr. Grandly looks about the wheelhouse, then says, "Captain Simpson, please take over the helm."

When Captain Simpson attempted to grab hold of the steering wheel, his hands passed through it as if it were a mirage. The mechanisms that controlled the vessel appeared to be devoid of substance, hollow, with no mass. And when Mr. Grandly, Bob, and John tried to apprehend Captain Black and First Mate Lance Monticello, they were unable to grab hold of them. This inexplicable energy or force that had protected the crew on the ramp in Woods Hole seemed to have held true for every crew member aboard the ferry. Their bodies appeared to lack physical mass, almost as if they were only images, astral projections.

After having exchanged a series of threats and counter-threats, coupled with the failed attempt to commandeer the ferry, the would-be mutineers were ordered out of the wheelhouse by Captain Black. However, by then, five crew members had arrived and escorted the men to the freight deck without incident.

Moments later, a small gaggle of passengers converged on Chairman Grandly and his co-conspirators, fearing that their hostile actions were an attempt to highjack the ferry.

Now banished from the wheelhouse, all they were left to do was roam around the freight deck and wait for the ferry to arrive at Vineyard Haven.

As soon as the ferry docked, Mr. Grandly, Bob, and Captain Simpson were escorted off the vessel. However, John had been asked by a member of the crew to remain on board so that Captain Black could have a word with him.

While standing upstairs on the deck, waiting for Captain Black to come out of the wheelhouse, John looked down at the dock and watched passengers and vehicles disembark from the ferry. Among the throngs of people, he happened to notice Mr. Grandly, Bob Cunningham, and Captain Simpson aggressively pushing their way through the crowd, shoving aside anyone who happened to stunt their forward progress. It was reminiscent of an icebreaker cutting a path through frigid waters in the Arctic Ocean. *No doubt they're in a hurry to get back to Woods Hole,* John thought.

Suddenly, the captain appeared. John hadn't noticed that he was standing next to him and was startled when he heard him speak.

"Hello, John. Thanks for staying aboard," the Captain said as he looked around quizzically, almost as if he were disoriented while attempting to get his bearings.

"Captain Black! I didn't realize you had come out of the wheelhouse," John said as he moved from leisurely leaning against the railing to suddenly standing straight up, his posture mimicking a soldier standing at attention. What can I do for you, sir?"

The captain smiled, and said, "John, please have a seat and allow me to explain."

"Explain what?"

"The reason the Islander and her crew from 1950 have come back."

At first, John felt overwhelmed as evidenced by the curious expression on his face. He couldn't quite grasp what the captain was alluding to. But then, he relaxed a bit and sat down on a deck chair next to the captain and gave him his undivided attention.

"You see, John, I had noticed something about you when you first came aboard. Then, it occurred to me that I remember seeing you decades ago, when you were just a young boy. I'll get to that in a minute. With respect to the issue at hand, I can see that you're unlike Mr. Grandly and Mr. Cunningham in that you seem to exude the qualities of a sincere, hardworking man. In addition to being honest and trustworthy, you possess a genuine compassion for your fellow human beings," he said.

At that point, John was puzzled. "I seem to possess *what*?" he asked.

"Compassion," he said. "You believe in doing right by others."

John nodded in agreement.

The captain continued.

"What it all boils down to, Mr. de Souza, is that good customer service is practically nonexistent today; it's gone the way of the dinosaur. Unfortunately, many businesses operate in this manner. They have only one goal in mind: to make as much money as possible. And in most cases, company CEOs and their management teams are gutless capitalists; they think nothing of fleecing their customers and taking their hard-earned cash. There's no equal exchange of value for money, particularly when it involves a service for which customers must pay. And the most egregious thing of all—and what bothers me most—is that there's no concern for the welfare of others, no conscience, no sense of dignity. It's nothing but a money-grab. And it's not just the Commonwealth Ferryboat Company that's guilty of this transgression. Countless other businesses operate in this manner. But, the fact that the C.F.C. chooses to engage in such behavior is an offense to me and the entire crew of the Islander," the captain said.

"Well, captain, if there's one thing you're right about, it's that I do care about our customers," John said.

"I know. Come to think of it, I remember seeing you aboard this ferry many times when you were just a boy in the early 1960s. You always seemed so excited to be here. John, I saw something special in you then, and I'm pleased to see that my assumptions were correct. You've become a great general manager at the C.F.C. Congratulations," the captain said.

"Thank you, sir."

"You're very welcome, John."

"Captain Black, may I ask you a question?"

"Sure," he said.

"What was your most memorable experience as captain of the Islander?"

The captain thought for a moment, and then said, "Well, my most memorable moment didn't occur while I was actually the captain. What I mean to say is that it took place prior to my assuming the helm of this glorious vessel."

"I don't understand," John said.

Captain Black said, "I used to be a huge movie buff, and, one of my favorite actors was James Cagney. I think I saw all of his movies. In fact, he once owned a house on the Vineyard. Somewhere up-island, if I remember correctly. He was a popular celebrity on Martha's Vineyard. Prior to when the Islander had come into service, James Cagney's daughter, Cathleen, had christened the ferry by smashing a bottle of champagne across her bow. To me, it was unimaginable that I had not only met Mr. Cagney, but that his daughter had played a role in the vessel that I'd spend my entire career on as its captain. Now, *that* was exciting!"

"I agree; that's some story," John said.

"I apologize for having digressed," the captain said. "Now, let me get back to the business at hand. The reason the Islander has returned is simple. We're here to restore something that's been lost over time."

"What's that?" John asked.

"Quality and exemplary customer service," Captain Black said. "You see, son, the C.F.C. has gone astray; it has become a shell of what it used to be. It once was a safe and dependable means of transportation to the islands at a reasonable price. That's what my crew and I had known and was one of the reasons we were proud to have worked for the C.F.C. But, unfortunately, it's now a laughingstock, motivated primarily by greed. Our purpose for being here now is to rectify the C.F.C.'s fall from grace. And, there's one other very important reason."

"What?"

"When the C.F.C. Board of Directors decided to retire the Islander, she had logged just under three-million nautical miles of service. And, if I'm not mistaken, she's twenty-six thousand miles short of that mark. My crew and I are here to see that she reaches that milestone. I guess you could say that it's also about pride," the captain said.

"So, what you're saying is that the Islander will continue to operate on the Woods Hole-Martha's Vineyard route until she has sailed three-million nautical miles?" John asked.

"That's correct. And mind you, there's nothing that the C.F.C. Board of Directors, State Police, Coast Guard, or the federal government can do to stop it. By now, you probably realize that," the captain said.

"But it'll take years to achieve that goal," John said.

"Six months, to be exact," the captain said.

"How's that possible?"

"Unlike what occurs today, the Islander can operate around the clock, twenty-four hours a day, seven days a week. By doing that, she'll achieve the goal in six months," the captain said. "Also, we've taken over the C.F.C. online reservation system. Customers can now make a reservation any time they'd like—twenty-four hours a day, seven days a week."

"But how could you possibly work around the clock? What about sustenance? What about sleep?"

The captain chuckled.

"We don't require either. You seem to have forgotten that we're not of this realm. As such, we're not subject to earthly needs, desires, or limitations," the captain said.

"Okay. But what about the supplies, fuel, and maintenance you'll need to operate the ferry?"

"With respect to those things...as the Good Book says: *Our cup runneth over.* We'll have all that we need to accomplish our objective," the captain said with a smile.

Though John was intrigued by all of this, he still found it difficult to reconcile the fact that it was actually occurring. Everything he had learned about physics and the natural order of the universe had been turned on its head. None of it made sense.

Captain Black glanced at his watch, and then said, "It's almost time to leave port. But before you go, here's what I'd ask you to do, John. No doubt the C.F.C. Board of Directors will continue its futile attempts to intervene. It would be helpful if you could somehow try to convince them that they'd be wasting their time and resources on such an endeavor."

"But, Captain, I have no authority or influence over what the Board of Directors decides to do. Besides, they'd never listen to me, anyway. In their eyes, I'm just a lowly general manager," John said.

"Well, John, I can assure you that after our work here is done, you'll have earned a level of respect that the C.F.C. has never seen before. You'll be in a position to do many great things, should you choose to do so," Captain Black said.

John, still unable to connect the dots, nodded his head as if he understood, but the blank expression on his face and far-away look in his eyes easily alerted the captain to the fact that he was not getting through to John. It was almost as if everything he had said had gone in one ear and out the other.

"Not to worry, John. You'll understand it all in time. Thanks for chatting with me. Now, if you'll excuse me, I must prepare for departure."

"Thank you, Captain Black," John said as he stood up from the chair and walked toward the stairs to the freight deck and made his way off the ferry.

Three short blasts sounded from the Islander's air-horn as she departed for Woods Hole. John walked into the ferry terminal and made his way up the stairs to the second floor. When he reached his office, he was surprised to see Mr. Grandly and Bob Cunningham plopped down in two chairs next to his desk.

"John! Bob and I were wondering what had happened to you. Where've you been?" Mr. Grandly asked.

"I was asked to stay aboard the ferry. Captain Black wanted to have a word with me," John said.

"About what?"

"He explained to me why the Islander has come back."

"Is that so? What did he say?" Bob asked.

At first, John hesitated. But then, while looking at them, said, "The Captain and his crew think that the C.F.C. is doing a disservice to its customers. And that the C.F.C.'s only interested in making money, turning a profit. That's one of the reasons they've come back."

"Oh? And what's the other reason, or reasons?" Mr. Grandly asked.

"When the board voted to retire the Islander, she had logged just under three-million nautical miles of service, and they're here to ensure that she reaches that mark." John said.

"Is that so? Well, if I have my way, that ferry won't sail another day because she'll be propped-up on stilts in dry-docking by tomorrow night," Mr. Grandly said, with defiance.

"According to Captain Black, there's nothing that you, I, or anyone else can do to stop them from carrying out their mission," John said.

Mr. Grandly wrenched his face and displayed an ugly scowl. He then waved his hands in a dismissive manner, as if to debunk what John had said.

"What else did he say? Not that it matters," Mr. Grandly insisted.

"He said that there's nothing we can do to stop what's happening," John reiterated.

"We'll see about that, Mr. de Souza," Mr. Grandly said in a recalcitrant tone. "There'll be an emergency meeting of the C.F.C. Board tomorrow at 6:00 p.m. in Woods Hole. Please plan to be there, John."

Another meeting? For what purpose? This guy seems hell-bent on engaging in feats of futility, John thought.

"I'll be there," John said.

"Good. We'll see you then. Come on Bob, let's go," Mr. Grandly exhorted.

John watched from his office window as the two men traipsed across the parking lot and boarded a freight barge about to depart for Woods Hole. He then shuffled to his desk and sat down to mull over what Captain Black had said. It all seemed so real, but how could it be?

After having navigated through an emotional day, John finally decided to pack it in. He grabbed his briefcase, walked out of the office and jumped into his car for the eighteen-mile trip home. About an hour later, while sitting at the dinner table, John appeared mum. He hardly uttered a word, an unusual trait for him, to be sure. In an attempt to break John out of his solemn mood, Elisa decides to initiate conversation.

"So, how was your day? Did anything unusual happen at work?" she asked.

John looks at Elisa with a forced, half-smile. But the eyes, being a window to the soul, revealed his true feelings.

"My day was just great, thank you. If you ignore the fact that I was aboard a ferry that no longer exists and had a conversation with a captain who's been dead since 1985, all in all, I'd say it's been a typical day at the office," John said.

"What on earth are you talking about, John?"

"I know it sounds crazy, Elisa. But what I'm saying is true. Somehow, the Islander has come back to life. At this very moment, she's sailing between Woods Hole and the Vineyard. Mr. Grandly, Bob Cunningham, Captain Simpson, and I were aboard her this morning. We actually traveled from Woods Hole to the Vineyard on the Islander," he said.

Elisa got up from her chair, walked over to John and gently placed her hand on his forehead. "No fever, but I wonder what's gotten into you," she said.

"Elisa, I'm not sick, and, I haven't gone insane. If you don't believe me, then I'd suggest we take a ride to Vineyard Haven after dinner. I want you to see it for yourself," John said.

"You want me to see what?"

"The Islander."

Wondering whether to take John seriously, or not, Elisa said, "Okay."

They quickly finished their meals, then hopped into the car and drove to the C.F.C. wharf in Vineyard Haven. Elisa had a vested interest in confirming, one way or another, whether her husband had gone completely berserk.

About twenty minutes later, while sitting in the car at the wharf, the Islander came into view. "Elisa, look! Do you see the ferry? She just rounded West Chop," John said.

Elisa looked toward West Chop, and at first, she was speechless. Several minutes later, as the Islander passed the breakwater and made its final approach to the dock, Elisa realized what John had said was, in fact, true.

"Well, I'll be. I don't believe it...you were telling the truth after all, John," she said.

They got out of the car and walked briskly towards the ramp to watch the Islander snuggle into the slip. After the vessel had been secured to the dock, Manny Barboza waltzed off the freight deck wearing the same bright smile that John had seen during his brief interaction with him earlier that day. Manny nodded and waved to them. John waved back, but then turned to Elisa and said, "Do you believe me now?"

All Elisa could do was to stand there in disbelief.

After watching the vehicles and passengers disembark from the ferry, John and Elisa returned to their car. And for the entire drive home, they remained silent, lost in their own thoughts.

As John maneuvered the car into the driveway, he said, "The C.F.C. Board of Directors is holding a meeting tomorrow evening, and Mr. Grandly made it quite clear that he wants me to attend.

"What's the meeting about?" she asked.

"Somehow, Mr. Grandly seems to think that the Islander can be stopped. But Captain Black had assured me that there's nothing that the board or anyone else can do. He even requested that I convey that message to the Board."

"Are you going to do it?"

"I don't know. But then again, I feel I have no choice but to do what the captain had asked. It's almost as if a higher power is compelling me to comply with his request."

"But why did he ask you?" she asked.

"Don't know that either. However, the captain said he remembers seeing me aboard the Islander when I was a boy. Also, he mentioned how he used to get a kick out of my reaction each time he saw me on the ferry and how enamored I was to be there. I guess that's one reason he had asked me to do his bidding," he said.

"That's quite an honor," Elisa said.

"Thanks a lot," John said with a smirk as he turned the key to the ignition and shut off the engine. They got out of the car, walked into the house and sat down at the kitchen table.

"To be honest, I've never felt as apprehensive about something as I do about this," John said. "Sometimes I think I should just resign from the C.F.C."

"You think you should quit? Why would you do that?" Elisa asked.

"You really want to know?"

"Yes."

"Well, it's mainly because I've lost faith in the Commonwealth Ferryboat Company. Since the Islander's return, I realize how stupid I've been for all these years, putting up with the bullshit and turning a blind eye to the untoward things that occur at the boat line," John said.

"Would it not make sense to do what Captain Black has asked? If you feel that strongly about it, then I can't think of a better reason to initiate a change for the better. You never know; something just might come of it," Elisa said.

John thought about what his wife had said. And then he said, "You're right, Elisa. Instead of calling it quits, I should do everything I can to make a difference. I'm going to that meeting tomorrow. And I don't care if the entire board thinks I'm crazy; I have to do the right thing, even if it costs me my job."

"Now, that's the John that I know and love," she said as she patted him lightly on the back.

"I'm exhausted; I think I'll call it a night," John said.

"I'm right behind you," Elisa said.

They climbed the stairs to the bedroom, and in less than ten minutes, they'd changed into their pajamas, washed their face and hands, brushed their teeth, and got into bed.

About an hour later, John suddenly awoke. He couldn't get the events that had occurred that day out of his mind. Unable to fall back to sleep, he got out of bed and snuck down the stairs to the living room as quietly as he could. He turned on the television, and with the volume turned down low, he clicked through the channels, only to realize that nothing of interest was on—just mindless infomercials, boring rebroadcasts of selectmen's meetings, and reruns of old westerns.

The TV is such an idiot box. How do people become so addicted to it? he wondered as he turned off the television and made his way back upstairs to bed.

Chapter Sixteen

The following afternoon, John, weary from lack of sleep, caught the 5:00 p.m. ferry to Woods Hole in order to make the C.F.C. board meeting by 6:00. While sitting next to a window inside the vessel, he looked out at Vineyard Sound and happened to see the Islander traveling in the opposite direction on its way to the Vineyard. He still couldn't believe that the Islander was chugging back and forth, non-stop, between Woods Hole and Martha's Vineyard. John hadn't prepared any remarks for the meeting because he decided to speak from the heart, to tell it like it is, the C.F.C. Board of Directors be damned.

Upon entering the boardroom, John could almost feel the tension in the air; it swirled around him like fallen leaves blowing in the wind on a cool, crisp autumn morning. A distinct feeling of uncertainty permeated the room; the camaraderie and friendly banter usually exchanged among the board members was conspicuously absent.

Even Mr. Grandly, known to be a well-dressed, debonair individual who exuded great confidence, appeared to be anything but. He looked haggard and disheveled. It was almost as if he had been beaten down to a point of destitution, a homeless man wandering the streets, begging passersby for a few coins to buy something to eat. In addition to looking as if he hadn't had a good night's sleep in weeks, his charcoal-gray sports jacket and matching slacks were wrinkled, rough-dry, as if he'd slept in them. A stubbly, five o'clock shadow covered his face like a tattered Halloween mask. It made him appear as if he were a convict who had escaped from prison and was on the run—a fugitive from justice—desperately attempting to avoid being apprehended by the authorities.

Two board members, conversing in one corner of the room, had suddenly stopped talking and made their way to their seats around a rectangular mahogany table. John walked over to a chair on the opposite side of the table and sat down next to Bob Cunningham.

Mr. Grandly called the meeting to order. He banged a gavel three times on the table, and said, "This meeting of the C.F.C. Board of Directors is now in session."

As the idle chatter quieted down to whispers, Mr. Grandly grabbed hold of a Styrofoam cup, raised it to his lips, and took a sip before placing it back down on the table.

"Good evening everyone. I want to thank you for being here at such short notice. As you all know, this meeting is extremely important. The future of the Commonwealth Ferryboat Company could very well rest on whether we successfully resolve this problem, or not," Mr. Grandly said.

He continued.

"As you know by now, we've been placed in the unenviable position of having to deal with something that you'd expect to see in a science fiction movie. In fact, if it were a movie, the title might be: *Return of the M/V Islander.*"

Not only could you hear a pin drop in the room, but expressions of disbelief, and, in some cases dismay, looked as if they had been chiseled on to the faces of several board members. It was akin to looking at the images of Presidents Washington, Jefferson, Roosevelt, and Lincoln etched in stone on Mount Rushmore.

"And for the non-believers who might find what I am about to convey to be preposterous, let me assure you that it is not. In fact, Mr. Cunningham, Mr. de Souza, Captain Simpson, and I have had first-hand experience to the contrary. By some extraordinary occurrence, the Islander seems to have risen from the dead. It's true that she's back. The four of us were aboard her yesterday," he said.

"Mr. Chairman, do you *really* expect us to believe that the Islander has actually come back after having been dismantled?" a board member asked.

"Mr. Walsh, where have you been for the past week, on another planet? This has been the lead story on just about every television network, not to mention the fact that it's in all the newspapers—*The Martha's Vineyard Times; Vineyard Gazette; The Cape Cod Times; Boston Globe; The Providence Journal,*" Mr. Grandly said.

Mr. Walsh looks at Mr. Grandly with a defiant expression, and says, "I've just returned from a two-week hunting and fishing trip to the White Mountains. I had no access to a cellphone, the Internet, e-mail, or any other form of communication. I received your message only when I got home late last night."

"Well, let me be one of the first to welcome you back. I hope you had an enjoyable trip, because now we've got a bigger fish to fry. In fact, it's a huge fish made of WWII surplus steel, and its name is the Islander," Mr. Grandly said.

Mr. Walsh smirked, as if he didn't believe a word of what the chairman had said. Mr. Grandly glanced around the room and noticed the solemn demeanor of the other board members. It seemed that the expression on everyone's face was pensive, reminiscent of a wandering flock of sheep, lost and unsure of which way to go, pining for someone or something to lead them out of a morass.

Grandly spoke. "Given the situation, we should admit that we've got a rogue ship on our hands. It must be dealt with; it must be stopped!"

"Yes, but how?" a board member asked. "You've told us about the difficulties that you, the State Police, and the Coast Guard have all had, and that nothing's been able to stop the Islander. If that hasn't worked, then what makes you think *we* can do anything?"

"That's a good question; it's the reason why I called you all here today. To be frank, I'm at a loss as to what to do, but we'd better come up with a solution. Otherwise, there'll be dire consequences for everyone, not to mention the effect it'll have on the Commonwealth Ferryboat Company," Mr. Grandly said.

"Bob, I had heard that you said that it was impossible to take control of the Islander because animate objects on the ferry were inanimate, including members of the crew? And that they couldn't be stopped or apprehended by State Police? Is that true?" another board member asked.

"Yes, it's true," Bob Cunningham said.

John de Souza sat in his chair and wondered if he should mention the conversation that he had had with Captain Black.

However, after vacillating for several minutes, he decided to remain quiet.

"Do you think we could use a blockade to stop the ferry?" a third board member asked.

"We'd need a fleet of ships to do that. Even if it were possible, it probably wouldn't work. There's something that's protecting the Islander and her crew," Bob said.

"We've got to do something, damn it!" Mr. Grandly said as he pounded his fist hard on the table.

As the meeting dragged on, it became more contentious. Tempers flared. Mr. Grandly's demeanor took a turn for the worse. He lashed out at the board members at the slightest disagreement and threatened them for expressing an opinion, something that the chairman had interpreted as being disloyal. The tension in the room had gotten to a point where no one dared to offer a suggestion for fear they'd be lambasted by Mr. Grandly.

"Well, does *anyone* have a suggestion as to what we should do?" Mr. Grandly asked, in a condescending tone.

Silence.

"Come on now, people. Has a cat gotten your tongues?" he asked.

John couldn't help but notice how everyone seemed to cower from Mr. Grandly's diatribe. John had had enough; he felt he had no choice but to speak up.

"Uh, excuse me, Mr. Grandly. I'd like to address the board, if I may," John said, as he raised his right hand.

Grandly stared at John, daggers in his eyes, and said, "And what is it you'd like to say, Mr. de Souza?"

"Well, sir, in my opinion, the solution to this dilemma is really quite simple," John said.

Suddenly, all eyes were fixed on John. Everyone seemed to hold their breath as they waited to hear what he had to say. It was almost as if he had possessed a sage wisdom, or divine truth that would save the myopic world of the Commonwealth Ferryboat Company.

Just as John was about to speak, the faint, low timbre of the Islander's horn sounded in the distance. No doubt she was carrying another load of passengers and vehicles from the Vineyard to Woods Hole.

Mr. Grandly seemed disturbed by the sound of the ferry's horn. It struck a nerve. It was a stark reminder that he, as chairman of the board, had to find a solution to the problem, lest he be deemed a failed leader.

Mr. Grandly nodded his head, and said, "Please continue, Mr. de Souza."

John took a deep breath, and said, "What I'm about to say might sound like something that's not possible. And afterwards, you might be inclined to not believe a word of it, or perhaps think that I belong in a mental institution. But I can assure you that everything I am about to say is true."

Suddenly, the room had become still; you could almost hear the faint hum of electricity flowing through the florescent light bulbs that were suspended from the ceiling. John looked around the room, then said, "For all the naysayers here tonight, let's get one thing straight. The Islander has returned, whether you choose to believe it, or not. I know this to be true, as does Mr. Grandly, Bob Cunningham, and Captain Simpson because we were aboard her yesterday. And let me make this perfectly clear: we were not aboard another boat; we didn't fly in an airplane or helicopter, and we certainly didn't swim across Vineyard Sound to get to the island. We traveled there on the Islander, period."

The board members looked quizzically at each other, expressions of incredulity and anxiety on their faces.

John continued. "After we arrived at Vineyard Haven, Mr. Grandly, Bob, and Captain Simpson were escorted off the ferry. But Captain Black, the skipper of the Islander, had asked a crew member to ask me to stay aboard because he wanted to have a word with me. During our conversation, the captain shared many things, one of which was the reason the Islander had come back from the great beyond, if you will."

Board member, Steve Sinitsky, suddenly interrupts John.

"Mr. de Souza, are you sure you hadn't been drinking yesterday or indulging in some illicit substance such as crack cocaine or LSD?" he said, snickering.

"No, I was not drinking, and I've never taken hallucinogens," John replied.

"Steve, what John says is true. Now, would you please let him continue?" Mr. Grandly said.

"Sorry," Steve said.

John spoke again.

"I've given a lot of thought to what the Captain had said. And though it's hard to admit, I'd have to agree with him. He told me that the Commonwealth Ferryboat Company is only a shell of what it used to be. Today, its mission is based on profit, nepotism, and a wanton disregard for the most valuable commodity that a business possesses, which is its customers."

He continued. "These days, the C.F.C. is morally bankrupt, steeped in financial malfeasance that's on par with the lowest of the low. As such, it's destined to fail and sink into obscurity, taking along with it the cronies and do-nothing employees that comprise its ranks. These are people who have sucked the lifeblood out of the C.F.C. And, as the saying goes:

'A fish rots from the head.' It's unfortunate that that analogy fits the C.F.C to a tee," John said.

Mr. Grandly, frustrated by what John had said, rudely interrupts him. "Mr. de Souza, now that's all well and good, but I think it's best to move forward with a plan to stop the ghost ship that we have on our hands. We need to take a different approach," he said.

"Chairman Grandly, as Captain Black had told me, there's no stopping what's happening—you already know this. So, why do you insist on being so adamant?" John asked.

Mr. Grandly's eyes narrowed as he glared at John, and then said, "I'm not going to allow some figment of my imagination to hold the C.F.C. hostage."

"Tell me, Mr. Grandly, when was the last time a figment of your imagination transported you across Vineyard Sound to Martha's Vineyard?" Bob Cunningham interjected.

Mr. Grandly slouched back in his chair in a manner that projected an air of desperation, the expression of helplessness embossed on his face. After pausing for a moment, John spoke again. "Also, I was told that the other reason the Islander has come back is to fulfill the goal of reaching three million nautical miles of service. The C.F.C. Board of Directors had retired her before that could happen. And from what I understand, she intends to reach that goal," he said.

Silence fell over the room.

"To conclude, I'd suggest we take Captain Black's advice and do what's best for our customers. Anything less would be a disservice. What's more, it wouldn't bode well for the C.F.C., its employees, or the Board of Directors," John said.

"Do you really think that it's prudent to take the advice

of a supposedly deceased ferryboat captain?" Board member, Dana Wilson, flippantly asked.

"You can make light of it if you so choose, Mr. Wilson. But be forewarned that you do so at your own peril," John said.

Mr. Grandly, teetering on the cusp of despair, sees that his plan to stop the Islander is falling on deaf ears. In a last ditch effort, he concocts yet another outlandish scheme to end the rogue ferry's activities.

"I'd like to propose that we use a military-style blockade to surround the ferry while she's docked. If that fails to stop her, then she should be destroyed," Mr. Grandly said.

John balked at the idea. The other board members, having now reached a point to where they were appalled, expressed their discontent through boisterous shouts. And, in the end, they unanimously agreed with John.

"You can't do that, Mr. Grandly," John said. "Not only is it not feasible; any attempt would most certainly fail because there's something else going on here. Somehow, the Islander is being protected. If I had to guess, I'd say its divine intervention—something that's preordained to which you have no control.

The board members nodded their heads in agreement.

"Divine intervention my ass!" Mr. Grandly said, interrupting John. "In case you've all forgotten, I'm the Board Chairman, and, as such, what I say ultimately goes."

"So, what you're saying is that you intend to supersede the Board's decision to not take action against the Islander?" a board member asked.

"That's correct," said Mr. Grandly. "And furthermore, since all of you seem to have lost the collective will to do your jobs—as if you're a bunch of useless wussies—I'm going to preempt these proceedings, right here, right now. From this point on, *I'll* make the final decision as to what we should do," Mr. Grandly said.

Suddenly, board member Dana Wilson, taken aback by Mr. Grandly's Caesarian-like attitude, felt compelled to speak up.

"Mr. Chairman, don't you think you're taking this shtick of yours a little too far?"

"Shut up, Wilson! I know exactly what I'm doing. Must I remind you that I'm the Chairman of the Board?" he said.

"No," Dana replied. "You've reminded us several times already."

"Well then, that settles it," Grandly said.

A third board member chimed in. "Mr. Grandly, regardless of what you decide to do, I'd still like to hear what Mr. de Souza has to say."

While several of the others had voiced their concurrence with Mr. Wilson's position, Mr. Grandly, red-faced and wearing a mean scowl, attempted to commandeer the conversation, but was unsuccessful.

John stood again, but, before he spoke, he tried to recall exactly what Captain Black had said. He then continued. "Customer service…it's all about providing exemplary customer service and doing whatever it takes to achieve that end," he said.

Mr. Grandly countered, "There you go again, John. When are you going to stop singing that same old, tired refrain?"

Surprised by Mr. Grandly's questioning, John rolled his eyes, and then stared at him as if he were a madman that had gone completely berserk.

Mr. Grandly, now openly defiant, stood up from the table. He looked around the room, and said, "We provide our customers with the best possible service and treat them with the dignity and respect that they deserve, given the resources we have, and that's that!"

Again, the board members fell silent. It was as if an epiphany had occurred among them all at once. They seemed to have understood what John was attempting to convey; it made sense.

John said, "No, you're wrong, Mr. Grandly. We *don't* provide our customers with the best possible customer service. In fact, I'm embarrassed by the lackluster service that we provide. To be frank…it sucks. We've much to do in that regard."

"Please continue, Mr. de Souza," another board member said.

"If the Commonwealth Ferryboat Company wants to regain the trust and integrity that it once had, then this board must change the manner in which it conducts business. Otherwise, the C.F.C. is doomed, like the Ford Etzel. And in order to avoid that fate, it would behoove the board to stop sitting on its hands and implement a service model that was witnessed yesterday aboard the Islander. Nothing less will do," John said.

John's comments seemed to have rung true to everyone, except for Mr. Grandly.

"What you're saying, John, is utter nonsense. It's a bunch of malarkey," Grandly sneered.

Much to the dismay of John and the C.F.C. board members, Mr. Grandly's obsession with stopping the Islander had reached a point to where he had become untenable.

"Listen, you bunch of spineless idiots. It seems as though none of you has the good sense or conviction you were born with. Can't you see what's at stake here? Why is it so difficult for you to support my directive? I hereby declare this Board to be inept. I'm moving ahead with a plan to stop the Islander even if I have to go it alone. This meeting is adjourned!" He then slammed the gavel down on the table, snapping off the head from the handle. Dumbfounded, John left the conference room, hopped on the ferry, and returned to the Vineyard.

Chapter Seventeen

Early the next morning, the Governor of Massachusetts, in coordination with the United States Department of Homeland Security and the Department of Defense, sent two U.S. Coast Guard cutters and two Navy warships to Woods Hole. Orders were to surround the Islander while she sat docked in the slip.

Meanwhile, the crew aboard the Islander went about their busywork, preparing to load passengers and vehicles onto the ferry. However, before any passengers were allowed to go aboard, the State Police had evacuated the ticket office, cleared the area, and cordoned off streets for several blocks.

The State Police had debriefed the Coast Guard and Navy personnel about the failed attempts to take the crew of the Islander into custody. They realized that was no longer an option. After the area had been secured, the Coast Guard made an announcement over a loudspeaker.

"Attention! Attention, Motor Vessel Islander. This is Commander Louis Barkley, from the United States Coast Guard. You are in violation of U.S. Maritime Regulations.

As such, you have no authority to operate in these waters. You are hereby ordered to stand down and disembark from the vessel with your hands up. If you do not comply, it will be considered a form of aggression and your vessel will be destroyed," the commander said.

Captain Black replied by way of a public address system aboard the ferry. "U.S. Coast Guard, this is Captain Sigmund Black of the Motor Vessel Islander. We have received your order and are unable to comply because we're on a mission sanctioned by a higher authority. Therefore, we must respectfully refuse to honor your request."

"Motor Vessel Islander, you have exactly ten minutes to stand down. Please acknowledge."

No response.

By now, Captain Black and his crew had gathered on the upper deck of the ferry to watch the Coast Guard and the Navy prepare to act. It was almost as if the crew had expected to see a Fourth of July fireworks display.

Ten minutes had come and gone. And with the ferry devoid of passengers, the Coast Guard and Navy locked their weaponry on the Islander.

"Motor Vessel Islander, this is your final warning," the commander said.

No reply.

Minutes later, the order was given, and they fired their artillery, a barrage powerful enough to have sunk a small fleet. But when the guns ceased fire and the smoke had cleared, the Islander sat in the slip, unscathed.

In a show of appreciation, the crew of the Islander erupted in raucous applause, whistling and cheering in response to what they had perceived to be an entertaining pyrotechnics display. Captain Black repeatedly sounded the Islander's air horn as a gesture of approval.

Mr. Grandly watched the failed attack from a safe distance. There was no mistaking the look of bewilderment on his face. He had no choice but to acknowledge that the jig was up; there was no stopping the Islander, or her crew. When Commander Barkley had informed Mr. Grandly that there was nothing more they could do, Mr. Grandly had finally decided to capitulate. As a result of this devastating defeat, he asked the State Police to stand down, remove the roadblocks, and allow people to return to the dock area.

Before long, the ticket office was again bustling with activity, and vehicles quickly filled the staging area to wait to board the next ferry. Thirty minutes later, the Islander departed Woods Hole and made yet another trip across Vineyard Sound to Martha's Vineyard.

News had spread quickly about the extraordinary events that had played out in Woods Hole. And John felt elated that the Islander had survived what could only be described as an all-out military assault on the vessel and her crew, precipitated by Mr. Grandly and his band of cronies.

John happened to be standing on the dock at Vineyard Haven when the Islander arrived, and, by the looks of the crew, it seemed as if nothing out of the ordinary had occurred. Like clockwork, the crew continued to do what they had been doing since they'd returned from who knows where.

No longer subjected to hostile takeover attempts, the Islander operated non-stop, twenty-four hours a day, seven days a week, until she reached the three-million nautical-mile mark of service to the Vineyard. At exactly six months to the day, after having achieved that important milestone, then, and only then, was the Islander ready to return to whence she came.

It was only by happenstance that John was at work the evening the Islander had departed Vineyard Haven for the final time. He didn't quite understand why, but something had compelled him to go down to the dock. When he arrived there, the ferry Islander was sitting in the slip, devoid of the constant activity that had become commonplace since she had returned.

It was almost as if the Islander and her crew had waited for John to appear before shoving off. Members of the crew stood on the freight deck of the vessel, its doors wide open, and gave him a final salute as the stout ferry pulled away from the dock. Captain Black sounded the low, throaty air horn and slowly piloted the ferry past the breakwater and out of the harbor.

Out of respect, John returned the salute, and, overwhelmed with feelings of melancholy, he watched the ferry navigate past West Chop and disappear from sight.

John walked back to his office, collected his briefcase, and slowly trudged to his car for what he expected to be a routine trip home. However, before he turned the key to the ignition and headed north on State Road toward Aquinnah, he sat there and thought about how empty he felt inside when the Islander sailed away the first time, only to be sold and dismantled for scrap. But here he was again, grappling with the same emotions. He felt as if he'd lost a dear friend, not once, but twice—a classic case of déjà vu.

Instead of making a right turn at Five Corners and heading up-island towards home, John took a left and drove to Oak Bluffs for what he felt was a much needed cocktail. When he arrived downtown, he slowly crept up Circuit Avenue in hopes of finding that elusive parking space. As expected, all of the spaces were occupied. Having become frustrated after driving around the block several times, he decided to drive to Ocean Park where he found several empty parking spaces.

John got out of the car, locked it, and walked back to Circuit Avenue, one block away. As he walked, the tantalizing aromas from restaurants, pizza parlors, and ice cream shops wafted in the air. Not one to be easily tempted by these culinary offerings, he continued up the street toward Cookie's Tap—a local bar that had been in business since he was a boy—where his parents had often patronized for many years. After he had arrived at the front door, it occurred to him that, for some reason, the walk from Ocean Park seemed to take less time than usual. Perhaps it was because he was preoccupied by thoughts of the Islander's departure, which made him feel downtrodden.

John sauntered into the small confines of Cookie's Tap—a dimly-lit cubbyhole—no windows, no frills—and sat on a stool at the bar. Ten small cocktail tables, surrounded by three wooden chairs each, were crammed into a space that was meant to accommodate no more than five tables. Tacky-looking beige tablecloths, frayed at the edges, were spread over the tables with scented candles with flames that flickered on top. A thick, blue haze, indicative of customers puffing on cigarettes, drifted about the room. The smoke burned John's eyes and nearly choked him each time he took a breath. And when the smoke converged with the pungent odor of alcohol and stale beer, it was almost too much to endure.

John couldn't surmise why the lights inside the establishment were turned down so low. But then, it dawned on him.

More than likely, management had made a point of keeping the lights dim so that customers wouldn't bolt for the exit if they happened to notice the cockroaches and black ants that scurried across the countertop or darting across the floor.

An old jukebox, wedged in one corner of the room, happened to play a record called: '*Tighter*', by a 1970s group, Alive N Kickin. The lyrics in the song were almost prophetic; for they accurately portrayed John's sullen mood.

How appropriate that that song should be playing, John thought.

What seemed strange about the song was that instead of describing the loss of love between a boy and a girl, the lyrics, in John's case, analogized the loss of an inanimate object, a ferryboat.

While waiting for the bartender, John reached into a chipped porcelain bowl on the counter and grabbed a handful of stale, picked-over peanuts that had turned soft due to the high humidity in the room. Without giving it much thought, he tossed a few peanuts into his mouth. But then, he thought, *Lord only knows where the fingers of those who had rifled through the bowl before me had been*. However, he felt famished, and the chance he'd contract a deadly disease didn't faze him in the least.

John sat at the bar for hours, oblivious of time, and drank at least four Scotch and sodas—he'd actually lost count—amidst the clamor of customers as they filtered in and out of Cookie's Tap. In the background, the jukebox continued to crank out a variety of songs from all genres, one after another, some from as far back as the big band era of the 1930s and 40s.

After having had more than his share of libations and noticing that the stench of cigarette smoke had only gotten worse, John had finally reached a point to where it was too much—not to mention that his clothes reeked from the smell of black tar and nicotine. He paid his tab, then stumbled to his car and drove home.

It was past midnight when John turned into his driveway. He snuck up the stairs and tip-toed into the bedroom, as was his custom, being careful not to disturb Elisa. He then eased into bed—his head spinning from overindulgence at Cookie's Tap—and fell into a deep sleep.

Chapter Eighteen

John suddenly wakes up and looks at the clock on the nightstand—8:30 a.m. "Shit! I overslept," he blurted out.

He didn't remember that Elisa had awakened him before she left for work. He jumped up, showered, got dressed, and then ran out the door and drove as fast as he could to his office in Vineyard Haven.

After he parked the car, he got out and looked around, pleasantly surprised to see that activities at the wharf appeared to be normal. All vessels were on schedule, including the Island Gold—which had been out of service for the past two weeks—and the number of vehicles waiting to board the next ferry was as expected for that time of day.

When John entered his office, the first thing he noticed was a stack of paperwork piled up on his desk. He sat down at the desk with every intention of sorting through the paperwork, but thoughts of the Islander crept into his psyche and distracted him. There were times he wasn't sure whether the events of the last few days had actually occurred. But his inner voice had told him that they had, in fact, taken place.

Also, he surmised it was true because his depressed state of mind made even the simplest task seem like a herculean effort; he lacked for any motivation. What's more, his emotions vacillated between elation and sadness. On the one hand, he felt overjoyed to have been in the presence of his favorite vessel again, but on the other, sadness seemed to overwhelm him, all because the Islander had returned to the great beyond. *Why couldn't she have stayed?* he wondered.

Later that morning, while Mr. Grandly was holed up in his office at the Woods Hole terminal, the telephone rang. He looked at the phone and, after the seventh ring, reluctantly picked it up and said, "Hello?"

"Resign your board chairmanship, Mr. Grandly. Or else, you'll soon become a long-term guest at the Bristol County House of Correction where you won't need those expensive suits and snazzy crocodile dress shoes that you love to shuffle around in. The only attire you'll be wearing is a standard-issue, orange jumpsuit with your own personalized serial number monogrammed on the front and back," said a mysterious voice, followed by a sadistic laugh.

"WHO IS THIS?" Mr. Grandly shouted.

'Click' went the phone. Mr. Grandly slammed the phone down and slumped back in his chair, a nervous wreck. His body had begun to shake at the thought of the illegal activity that he had engaged in during the procurement process for the new ferry, Island Gold. *Is the jig up? Will what I had done finally be exposed?*

At 3:30 p.m., John boarded a ferry to Woods Hole to attend the C.F.C. Board Meeting. Much to his surprise, when he arrived there, Mr. Grandly was well-groomed and meticulously dressed, contrary to what John had expected to see. However, there seemed to be something weighing heavily on Mr. Grandly's mind. His mannerisms mimicked someone who had committed a serious crime and had been caught in the act. He fidgeted in his chair like a hyperactive child suffering from ADHD, in desperate need of a dose of Ritalin.

John waited for someone to broach the subject of the Islander. But no one did. Also, he noticed the chaos and confusion that had overshadowed the last C.F.C. Board meeting was conspicuously absent. There were no expressions of worry or despair on anyone's face. And the refreshments—sandwiches, Danish, assorted cookies, and beverages—were consumed in no time, just as they had been before the issue concerning the Islander had occurred.

John looks around the room, confused. The meeting was almost over, and he couldn't understand why the topic of the Islander hadn't been raised. Ten minutes before the meeting adjourned, John raises his hand and asks to be recognized.

"Yes, Mr. de Souza. Would you care to address the board?" Mr. Grandly asked.

"Yes, I would, Chairman Grandly," he said.

"The Board recognizes Mr. de Souza," Grandly said.

"Thank you, Mr. Grandly. Uh, yes. I was wondering about the Islander," John said.

"The Islander? What about the Islander?" Mr. Grandly asked.

"Well, I was wondering what the Board has decided to do about her, if anything," John said, in a meek tone.

Suddenly, the room became quiet, all eyes looking squarely at him.

"John, would you mind telling us what you're referring to? Don't you remember that the Islander was scrapped last week?" Mr. Grandly said.

Last week? he thought. "I know she was scrapped, but I thought she had..."

"You thought she had what, John?"

"Nothing," he said as he pulled on a thread that dangled from his shirtsleeve.

"Are you feeling all right, John?" Bob Cunningham asked.

"Yes, I'm fine, Bob—thanks," John said.

"Are you sure?" Mr. Grandly asked.

"Yes," John said.

John, embarrassed, sat slouched down in the chair, wishing that he could disappear. W*as it all just a dream? Did none of this actually occur?* he thought to himself.

"Before we adjourn, I have some very important news to share," Mr. Grandly said.

The chatter in the room suddenly died down to a whisper.

"At this time, it is with mixed emotions that I announce my resignation as Chairman of the C.F.C. Board of Directors, effective immediately," Mr. Grandly said. "Serving as board chairman has been one of the most rewarding experiences of my professional career. But now, I feel it's time for me to retire. I have some personal endeavors that I'd like to pursue. Because of this, the time is right for me to step down as chairman of the C.F.C. Board."

A collective gasp spread through the room, a reaction to the unexpected news that the chairman had shared.

"Furthermore, after having given it much thought, I'd like to nominate Mr. de Souza to assume the chairmanship. That is, if you'd be willing to accept it, John."

John almost choked on his saliva.

Though it had come as a complete shock to everyone, most of all to John, he was tapped by Mr. Grandly to replace him as the C.F.C. Board Chairman. But John wanted no part of that responsibility. He preferred to remain in his job as general manager. What's more, rather than have to travel to and from the Vineyard to Woods Hole and back again each day—not to mention being locked away in a stuffy office above the C.F.C. ticket office, making decisions that oftentimes fly in the face of what good customer service entails, John preferred to have direct contact with customers, something he had always enjoyed doing.

However, after mulling over the proposition, John decided to take advantage of the opportunity to act as interim Chairman of the Board until a permanent replacement for Mr. Grandly could be found. Throughout the twelve months that John had served as acting chairman, he implemented many improvements at the C.F.C. and consistently strived to achieve excellence, just like in days of old. And, in time, he, along with a new chairman, the board members, and his management team, had successfully turned the flagging operation around and accomplished what at one time was thought to have been an impossible task. The C.F.C.'s reputation was gradually restored, reminiscent of when the M/V Islander sailed majestically across Vineyard Sound. It was a time when good customer service was tantamount to a great legacy, a goal that any reputable business should strive to achieve each day.

Chapter Nineteen

Not long after Mr. Grandly had abruptly resigned as chairman of the C.F.C. board, John received a telephone call from his brother-in-law, Ralph.

"Good morning, John de Souza speaking. How can I help you?" he asked.

"Hello there, John. This is Ralph."

"Good morning, Ralph. How's it going? How's the new job?" John asked.

"All is well with me, thanks. The job is going great. I was fortunate to have found another employment opportunity after the Mississippi Dry -Dock Company had declared bankruptcy and went belly-up. Jacques Windham, the company's CEO, not only lost a lawsuit brought by three shipbuilders and was ordered to pay millions of dollars in restitution, but he was also convicted on a bunch of state charges and sentenced to serve ten years at the Massachusetts Correctional Institute in Shirley, Massachusetts.

"What a story," John said.

But the *real* question is how are things going for *you*? I had heard that when Mr. Grandly left the C.F.C., you became the interim Chairman of the Board. Is that true?"

"Yeah, it's true," John said.

"I also heard that Massachusetts Senate President, William Clay, was removed from office on a recall vote," Ralph said.

"Yes. He was forced out after having been indicted on corruption charges.

"And what ever became of Mr. Grandly?" Ralph asked.

"Not long after having stepped down, he was charged with conspiracy. However, he worked out a plea-bargain deal with the district attorney. He ended up testifying as a witness for the prosecution in the cases against Clay and Windham. For his cooperation, he received a reduced sentence."

"How much time did he get?" Ralph asked.

"Two years in the slammer, and five years' probation. However, I believe he'll be eligible for parole after one year. Can you believe that Mr. Grandly was involved in such a scheme?" John asked.

"I most certainly can. That low-down, no good swindler got exactly what he deserved. I had always had a feeling that, at some point, he'd be forced to resign," Ralph said.

"Forced to resign? I was under the impression that Mr. Grandly's departure was voluntary. He said that he was retiring," John said.

Ralph said nothing.

"Ralph, let me ask you something."

"Sure."

"You wouldn't happen to know who it was that dropped a dime on Mr. Grandly, would you," John asked.

Silence.

"Ralph?"

"Yes?"

"Well?" John asked.

"As the old saying goes, John, *'those that know don't tell, and those that tell don't know.* And I'll leave it at that," Ralph said.

"That's all you have to say about it?" John asked.

"Yes," Ralph said.

"Okay, thanks, Ralph."

"Thanks for what? I've done nothing."

"Okay, Ralph, if you say so. When are you coming back to the Vineyard?"

"Not until next summer. Tell my sister that I'll give her a call next weekend."

"Will do, Ralph. Take good care," John said.

"Good-bye," Ralph said.

For the next fifteen years, John de Souza remained on the job as general manager, during which time he had assumed additional responsibilities and helped transform the C.F.C. into a business that had once again earned the respect and admiration of its customers, employees, and business associates.

When John retired from the Commonwealth Ferryboat Company, he spent his newfound leisure time on Martha's Vineyard doing some of the things he used to do when he was a young boy, such as swimming, fishing, and riding a bicycle to the Vineyard Haven wharf to watch the ferries come and go.

The Motor Vessel Islander—the stalwart ferryboat from an era gone by—provided customers with safe passage between Woods Hole and Martha's Vineyard for fifty-seven years. And though her brief return was only in John's imagination, it nevertheless acted as a catalyst that fostered the resurrection of a long-lost commodity at the Commonwealth Ferryboat Company, which was trust, goodwill, and, of course, exceptional customer service.

About the Author

Kevin Parham is the author of the award-winning memoir: *The Vineyard We Knew–A Recollection of Summers on Martha's Vineyard;* mystery novel: *Keeper of the East Bluff Light;* and autobiographical novel: *Westville.*

After having had a rewarding career as a professional musician, Kevin decided to pursue his passion for writing.

M/V Islander–Resurrection is Kevin's fourth book.

Connect with Kevin:

BLOG: *https://kevinjparham.wordpress.com/*
TWITTER: *https://twitter.com/Kevin_Parham14*
GOOGLE+: *tvwk9145@gmail.com*

Upcoming Releases by Pria Publishing

Orange Line to Forest Hills
Black Soul-White Skin
Libby the Owl

Indie-authors appreciate the support of their readers. If you happened to enjoy this novella, then please tell a friend or share it with someone. It's also helpful when an author receives a candid review. Please consider posting one on your favorite literary platform such as Amazon, Goodreads, etc.

To receive notifications about events and new releases, please feel free to sign-up for our newsletter at *www.priapublishing.com.* We respect your privacy and will never share or sell your contact information.

Made in the USA
Middletown, DE
17 May 2021

Made in the USA
Middletown, DE
17 May 2021

39104230R00116